EVEN CLOSER THAN THE SEA AND OTHER STORIES

BY

KYLE FISKE

Glenda,
Thanks so much for picking up the book, and I'm glad you enjoyed the stories!
Kyle

Even Closer Than the Sea and Other Stories

This is a work of fiction. Names, characters, businesses, places, events and incidents are either the products of the author's imagination or used in a fictitious manner. Any resemblance to actual persons, living or dead, or actual events is purely coincidental.

Cover photographs courtesy of NASA/JPL-Caltech/SSI and Library of Congress Prints and Photographs Division

ISBN 978-1535388375

TABLE OF CONTENTS

Introduction

For any aspiring writer of fiction, one fundamental question always presents itself: what should you write about? "Write what you know" is advice often given, and there are certainly advantages to that approach. When you have first-hand experience with a job, a relationship, a locale, a skill, an ideology, or what have you, it will be much easier to portray those things in a realistic, believable manner without doing a great deal of research or guesswork. Making any glaring factual errors in your descriptions or details becomes much less likely. Conversely, though, if you limit yourself only to subjects that you have first-hand knowledge of, the boundaries of your writing will be limited by the boundaries of your own life. And no matter how exciting or varied a life one has lived, it *is* only one life—and one lived in a finite temporal and physical space.

For many writers, their approach is simply "write what you like," and "write what you'd like to read." That's generally the route I take. If the subject is something that I actually do have personal and immediate knowledge of, all the better. Real life often gives you experiences simultaneously odder and more authentic than any you might be able to imagine, and when you're able to work those details into your writing, it can help to impart a sense of unique personality to the characters and veracity to the story. On the other hand, I would argue, part of being a writer of fiction is to put yourself in the shoes of people far different than you, and in situations and environments that you've never actually experienced. I find that the great fun of writing is trying to find that compelling, satisfying balance between the two.

I think my first memory of any type of storytelling that really captured my imagination was a television show. I grew up out in the country, on a farm in northern New York State, not far from the Canadian border. In those pre-cable days, our rooftop antenna was able to pick up about five or six stations—and even those not always clearly. One of those stations was good old CFCF 12, out of Montreal. I don't remember the first episode I saw, but I do remember being four years old, sitting on the couch and holding my big stuffed frog every Saturday morning, waiting excitedly for...ULTRAMAN! Ultraman was a half-hour Japanese television program, produced in the mid-1960's by many of the same people that made the Godzilla movies. The show followed the adventures of the Science Patrol, a quasi-governmental department whose agents, smartly outfitted in orange uniforms and equipped with laser guns and futuristic aircraft, would investigate and battle giant monsters and aliens—the type that seemed to be threatening Japan on a near-daily basis in the 1960's. This program absolutely captivated me.

From then on, it seemed I was always drawn to fantasy, science fiction, horror, westerns, martial arts, or any combination thereof, in any kind of media. I was nine years old in the summer of 1977, and for a boy of that age, seeing Star Wars for the first time on a big screen was a near-religious experience. I became equally enamored with the original Star Trek television series, shown heavily in reruns at the time. In the early 1980's, cable television came to our area, and I was exposed to a whole new world. Television shows like The Twilight Zone and The Outer Limits became my favorites, as well as Hammer horror movies, Japanese science fiction films, Shaw Brothers martial arts movies, and Italian westerns. Later on, I came to appreciate *film noir*, vintage American westerns, and classic Japanese samurai movies.

On the literary front, I started reading Marvel and DC comics at a very young age, then added Star Trek and Star Wars novels, and works by Jules Verne and Louis L'Amour, among others. In high school and college I became a fan of Poe, Lovecraft, Hemingway, and popular writers including Arthur C. Clarke, Ray Bradbury, Elmore Leonard and Stephen King. As an adult I've become extremely fond of both the fiction and non-fiction of Christian writers such as C.S. Lewis, G.K. Chesterton and J.R.R. Tolkien.

Along with all of these influences, one other factor greatly shaped my imagination and creativity. Growing up in the country, on a farm of 110 acres, I spent a good deal of time as a child just by myself, out in the woods and pastures. I think the impact of the natural environment on a young mind can't be overstated. For me, the various parts of the farm became stand-ins for different fictional environs. The small brook with the thick vegetation on either side became the African jungle, where Tarzan might have faced his foes. The dry pasture, where the sheep had eaten the grass right down to the ground, became the cowboy-filled deserts of the Southwestern U.S.; the thorny weeds that grew there which the sheep wouldn't eat (we called them "picker bushes") became cactus, and the small, dusty sheep-paths became cattle trails. The surrounding woods, filled with pines, maples, cedars and all kinds of brush, became the primeval forests of old Europe. And everything became Alaska, the North Pole, or Hoth in the frigid, snow-covered winters of Northern New York. Surveying the landscape with my trusty Daisy Model 95 BB gun in hand, I imagined all kinds of scenarios and adventures—and years later

I'm still imagining them.

Of the eleven stories in this collection, "The First Snow of the Season" is the oldest, written around 2002, as I recall. I wrote pretty sporadically over the next ten years or so, and then began focusing more on short stories around 2012. The most recent story of this collection is "A Girl in Trouble", written in early 2016.

These stories embody many of the influences I've mentioned above, both in subject and tone. In my writing you'll find a good deal of pulp adventure, action, classic sci-fi and atmospheric horror, along with some humor, a little theology—and not much graphic violence. I don't live out in the country any more, but I do live close to the ocean on the New England coast, and I'm not sure it's possible for any type of artist to live by the sea and not be influenced by it. Several of my tales in this collection reflect that setting.

Are these stories largely examples of escapism? I suppose they are, but I don't find that term to be particularly derogatory. As C.S. Lewis said to Arthur C. Clarke, "Who are the people most opposed to escapism? Jailors!" At any rate, thank you for reading these tales, and I hope my stories give you a thrill, a chuckle, and maybe a little glimpse of what might be stirring just under the calm surface...

The First Snow of the Season

Owen Denham pulled his wool cap down over his ears as the crisp, early November wind blew the first snowflakes of the season in off the ocean. The days were getting shorter, and already what little sun there was on this cloudy day was beginning to fade. Despite the lack of snow, the temperature had been below freezing for a week now, and the frost-crisped pasture crackled softly under his boots. Twenty-three, twenty-four, twenty-five...the lambs were all there. Thirty-one, thirty- two...all the ewes. Two, three, and...one of the rams was missing. Owen counted the flock again, but still he couldn't find the absent buck.

Where did you go? Owen tried to focus as he scanned the pasture in the soft, graying dusk.

The flock was moving past him up towards the hill to the barn, and they seemed to Owen to be a bit more anxious than normal. The usual relaxed, contented "baas" as the sheep made their way to the barn from the final grazing of the day were replaced by a nervous, half-swallowed bleating. Owen noticed that the sheep seemed less wary of him than usual, as well; they seemed intent on getting to the barn with as little fuss as possible, and by the most direct path available.

Owen looked back up the hill to his grandparents' house. The lights were on in the kitchen, and he knew that his mother and grandmother were busy making supper. His grandfather Elmer would probably be back from his trip to the feed store in town, if he hadn't stopped by the pub. Owen thought that it would probably be easier to go up to the house and get his grandfather to come down and help him look for the ram, but this was the first week that he had been allowed to do the chores by himself. He didn't want Grandpa Elmer to think that he couldn't handle the situation.

He looked back out towards the pasture and to the small but thick grove of oaks that jutted out from the main woods. The snow was beginning to fall more heavily now, and Owen was vaguely aware that the dull gray sky would be giving up the last of its light before long.

There was something moving in the trees.

Owen squinted through the gray, and he thought he could make out some movement in the brush under the oaks. There were some brush-entangled rolls of wire down there, from an old fence that his grandfather had taken down years ago, and Owen quickly figured that the ram had probably gotten himself tangled in one of those. The subtle satisfaction of having reasoned out a logical explanation for the missing buck boosted Owen's confidence, and with crook in hand, he began down the hill towards the grove of oaks.

***

Spending the first twelve years of his life in the suburbs of Ottawa, Owen didn't have much experience with the farming life, but he had taken to it easily. He had found the change of surroundings to be quite exciting. He would always remember the day that his parents had called him and his little sister into the living room on that bitterly cold day the previous March. His father was a pilot in the Royal Canadian Air Force, and his fighter wing was being called up to be sent to England. The war probably wouldn't last very long, Owen's mother said, but his father's stern gaze and grim, tight-lipped expression didn't support his mother's assertion. Hitler had to be stopped sometime, his father said, and better to do that in Europe than over here.

Owen's little sister began crying softly.

"How long will Daddy be gone?" she asked her mother, who pulled her close and wrapped her arms around the sobbing girl.

"It'll seem like no time at all," Owen's mother said, forcing back her own tears. "And we're going to stay with Grandma and Grandpa down in Massachusetts. Out in the country, you'll make new friends and have all kinds of fun things to do."

"It will be a nice vacation for all of you," Owen's father said. "Aunt Lynn is going to take care of this house while we're gone, and we'll probably all be back for Christmas."

Owen could sense that his father was fighting back his own emotions. The elder Denham turned and walked back towards the kitchen, gently squeezing Owen's shoulder as he walked by.

Owen had a keen interest in politics and the news of the world, and he had already discussed the whole situation with his father over the previous weeks. Owen liked the fact that his father didn't talk down to him as a child, but rather pushed him to think about the events and goings-on in the world and to understand them in more depth. He often smiled to himself and was secretly proud when his father would be discussing politics with some of his friends on a much simpler level than he did with Owen—and in the middle of their discussion his father would cast a wink to his son.

Although he was sad to leave his home in Ottawa and to see his father go overseas, the long train trip to Ipswich, Massachusetts had been quite enjoyable. His grandparents had been waiting for them at the railway station in Beverly, and he remembered the warmth he felt at seeing his Grandpa Elmer standing tall in his dark brown, old-fashioned topcoat, leaning slightly on his walking-stick ("don't ever call it a cane," his grandmother had told him when they last talked by phone, "always call it a walking-stick.") As Owen and his mother and sister walked towards the older couple, his grandmother opened her arms and with a welcoming smile on her face walked briskly towards them. His grandfather stayed where he was, the only emotion displayed being his bemused, contented smile and nod. Owen's sister Sarah ran into her grandmother's arms, but Owen ran past her to give his grandfather a hug. The elder man held Owen closely and tightly.

The ride back to his grandparents' farm was not far, but after the long train ride both his mother and his sister drifted off to sleep. Owen sat in the front seat as his grandfather drove, and he listened as Grandpa Elmer pointed out the scenery and neighbors they passed. Owen tried very hard to stay awake and pay attention to his grandfather, but as the car's heater gradually warmed up, Owen was vaguely aware that the sounds of the car and his grandfather's voice were cutting in and out, and then sleep was upon him. He woke up the next day in his new bed in his new room, and then later he got the whole tour of the farm. In the following weeks, he settled in quite comfortably to his new life.

***

Owen caught another glimpse of movement in the trees as he got closer, but it was getting too dark to see anything very clearly. He glanced back again up to the soft, warm lights of the house and barn. A damp mist was settling in with the cold over the pasture to his right, and the bleating of the sheep back in the barn seemed muffled and distant. Owen focused again on the stand of trees, still some fifty yards down the pasture. A clink of metal cut softly through the moisture-heavy, cold air. Owen stopped and cocked his head. He wasn't exactly sure whether the sound had come from in front of him or back from the barn. He gripped his gnarled, wooden crook a bit tighter, and he started again towards the grove of trees. *It was probably the rattling of that ram caught in the roll of wire.* Even as he got within twenty yards of the trees, the shadows and fading light made it difficult to see any details among the oaks and underbrush of the grove. Owen wasn't exactly feeling scared at this point, but his senses were keen and highly focused. He stopped and listened. He heard the metallic rattling sound again, more clearly—and this time he was sure it was coming from the trees up ahead. Owen's trepidation and uneasiness began to fade a bit, as everything now seemed to be falling into its logical place. It *had* to be the ram caught in the wire. He picked up his pace, moving towards the left, to the back side of the grove where the largest oak was. The briars and underbrush were thick, and wild grape vines were intertwined in a few of the white birches and other smaller trees. Owen pushed through these, ducking his head and shielding his eyes to avoid the resilient branches of the dense brush.

"All right, let's get you out of here," Owen said to himself as he pushed through to the big oak. He stopped. The image before him wasn't what he had expected. The rolls of wire were indeed under the tree, but there was no sheep caught in them. Owen looked up. On the large, lowest branch of the oak, about eight feet up from the ground, was draped the limp body of the missing ram. Its broken neck was twisted unnaturally against its shoulder, and the dead, open eyes looked blankly out towards the pasture. Through the cold autumn air, Owen heard the crackling of the brush to his left as something—something big—moved in slowly towards the oak.

Owen was aware of his body tensing of its own accord, and his breathing became shallow. It was now dark enough that he had trouble seeing anything distinctly through the underbrush. The crackling of the brush moved steadily closer, and Owen found himself stepping backwards. The snapping and popping of the brush was now directly behind the big oak. Owen's pulse was racing, and he could feel his body urging him to turn and run, but he found himself fixed in place by some subtle combination of paralysis and curiosity. He quickly looked up again at the lifeless face of the ram. The ram's head slowly straightened and turned towards him, the cold eyes fixed in their dull gaze. The unnaturalness of this action momentarily caused Owen's senses to reel, until he realized that the ram was being pulled off the limb from behind the tree. The face of the ram, resting on its fully outstretched front legs, receded steadily from Owen's view, into the darkness of the shadows and brambles behind the tree. Owen stood transfixed. The big ram's front hooves were still hanging about five feet above the ground as it swung into view again. As the ram sagged limply to the right of the tree, towards the pasture, Owen could finally see what was holding the dead animal.

It was easily nine feet tall, and it walked on two legs; on some level Owen instantly ruled out the possibility that it was a man of any sort. Its color seemed to be a dull, reddish gray, but the shadows and fading remains of the daylight made it difficult to tell for sure. It might have appeared a brighter red in the daylight, but Owen instinctively sensed that it was probably not often seen under those conditions. He could see the muscles of the thing's massive upper arms flexing and tensing as it maneuvered the ram out of the tree, and finally swung it over its shoulder. The thing turned to make its way out of the grove as Owen stood mesmerized. Its lower body seemed to be a bit darker colored than the upper body, and the feet struck Owen as particularly strange: almost like a thicker version of a bird's three-toed talon. Although its legs seemed proportionally short, it registered somewhere in Owen's mind that the stride of the thing's first step had to be no less than six feet. As the fantastical shock of this scene began to diminish ever so slightly, and Owen's senses began to adjust and accept that this thing was indeed real, the fear rose in him. The thing did not seem to have seen him yet. Owen felt himself stepping slowly backward, and he half-sensed the dried, partially frozen branch under his right foot as he began to slowly step back. It was too late to shift his balance forward, and the weight of Owen's step caused the branch to snap dully in the still, heavy, twilight air. Over the past few moments, Owen's quiet breathing and heartbeat seemed frighteningly audible to him; this was a thunderclap. The thing stopped and turned. Owen froze, but he could not look away from the thing. He couldn't distinctly make out the creature's face, but the eyes underneath its protruding, furrowed brow shone keenly and met Owen's gaze. The moment seemed to be as frozen as the ground under Owen's feet as the two stood staring at each other. Owen was vaguely aware of the limp front legs of the huge ram swinging listlessly as the frigid wind blew slowly but heavily through the grove.

The snow was falling more steadily now, softly muffling the natural acoustics; Owen's pulse seemed to beat with an increasing heaviness. The thing's expression was not one of hostility; it seemed to gaze at Owen with a detached indifference, and, Owen felt, perhaps even curiosity. It turned and adjusted the ram over its shoulder, and then walked away out of the grove and into the pasture. Owen watched it take its massive, steady strides until it disappeared across the field and into the enveloping shroud of the mist and nightfall.

***

Owen couldn't quite remember whether he had slowly walked or frantically run back up to the house, but the next thing he knew he was coming up the front steps to the kitchen. He didn't have his crook with him anymore; he must have dropped it somewhere along the way, although he didn't remember when. His grandmother and his little sister were standing over a steaming pot on the stove, and his mother was over at the counter, peeling potatoes. She glanced up as Owen came in.

"Hurry up and change your clothes, Owen. Supper'll be ready pretty soon," she said pleasantly as she furrowed her brow and looked down at the pots, trying to keep track of everything she had going. "Did you get all your chores done?" she asked, as she wiped her hands on her blue and white plaid apron.

"Yeah, all done," Owen said steadily, if remotely.

"Now hurry up and put those clothes in the cellar—I don't want this house smelling like the barn. And I hope you rinsed those boots off before you came in," she said, with more of a sense of routine than with any real annoyance.

Owen went through the kitchen over to the cellar door and went downstairs. He slid his shoulders out of his heavy coat, put his right boot in the bootjack and slipped the boot off. He finished taking off his other boot and put it on the rack, and he stood there in his sock-feet. The oil furnace kept the cellar almost unbearably warm, but after the events in the cold, dank air of the pasture, the heat felt soothing and seeped softly, steadily and deeply into his bones. He stood still for a moment as little bits—and some bigger bits—of his ordeal crashed haphazardly back into his mind. The warm, familiar surroundings he now found himself in seemed far removed from the fantastical events of the previous hour, but Owen was already accepting the fact that what had happened in the pasture was every bit as real as the low hum of the furnace next to him.

"Your bath is ready, Owen," his mother called from the top of the cellar stairs.

"Okay. Thanks, Mom," Owen replied.

Owen took his bath, dried, and put on the clean pair of dungarees and his everyday red flannel shirt that his mother had laid out for him on the floor next to the bathroom door. He went out to the living room where Grandpa Elmer was sitting by the fire, reading his newspaper. Owen sat down on the floor to the right of the fireplace, leaning against the empty old oak rocker, and he stared blankly into the flames. The bath, and the warmth of the fire had dulled much of the fear and shock, but the sequence of events that had occurred in the pasture were replaying themselves again and again just under the surface of his thoughts.

“Get everything done, Owen?” his grandfather asked, without looking up from his paper.

On some level, Owen did hear the question, but Elmer’s low, gentle voice blended with the sounds of the house gently creaking in the blowing wind, the rustle of his newspaper, the crackling of the fire and the voices and laughter of the women in the kitchen.

“Owen?” his grandfather said, looking up from his paper, a hint of concern crossing his face. He looked at the boy. “You’re white as a sheet, son,” he said. “What’s the matter?”

“Nothing,” Owen said. “I was just thinking about stuff.”

The older man fixed his eyes sternly on Owen. Something was not right. “What happened?” he asked, in a tone which was gentle, but demanded a response.

Owen paused for a moment before answering. “I saw something. Down in the pasture…something...” Owen trailed off.

“What was it?” Grandpa Elmer asked.

“Some kind of animal. It...killed one of the rams and...took it. I saw it. I think it was a bear or something...” Owen tried to adopt the tone that he had heard his father use in difficult situations, but he could feel that he wasn’t doing it very well. He knew that his grandfather loved and trusted him, but he was determined not to sound like a frightened child with a silly, vivid imagination. Adults have to deal with things like this now and then, he told himself, although a part of him knew that this situation was not part of the normal experience of anyone, adults included.

The elder man continued to look Owen in the eye. “Huh. There haven’t been too many bears around for quite a few years. Since I was a boy, really. You’re sure it was a bear?”

"I…I don't know, grandpa. It was getting dark. I couldn't see that clear," Owen said.

"Owen, *what did you see*?"

"I just don't know. It was big…really big. It...it walked on two legs. It was gray, I think, or maybe red. It didn't have any hair...it was kind of like leather...or an elephant's skin...or something. I don't know." Owen knew his voice was shaking, and he could feel the tears welling up.

The older man paused and looked down, and then he met Owen's eyes. "You didn't get too close to it did you? Are you all right, Owen? Did it...?"

"No," Owen said, trying to reign in his sobbing, "it...it didn't pay any attention to me." He paused, breathed deeply and calmed himself as best he could. "I...I didn't do anything, Grandpa. I was so scared, I could hardly move. I didn't know what to do."

Owen's grandfather sat back in his chair, and turned his gaze back to the crackling fire. "So, it's back," he said. "I thought maybe it was gone for good."

"You've seen it?" Owen asked. He leaned forward, eager to hear more, and also with a sense of relief; he knew his grandfather believed him.

"Yes, I've seen it." The older man paused, collecting his thoughts and considering the gravity his words might carry to a young boy. "It was back in '15, I think," he said, as he took another draw on his pipe. "Your grandmother and I had just bought the place and moved here. We had started our little farm, gotten a few head of sheep, and a few cows. We were doing well. You didn't need many animals to make a living at that time. Then we started losing some sheep. You expect to lose some, to coyotes, or maybe some stray dogs that have got the taste of blood–but that wasn't the case. A coyote would always take the lambs first, or the old ewes—they always go for the weakest. But this thing never took any lambs or ewes. It was always the strongest bucks." The older man continued staring into the fire.

"What did you...see?" Owen asked.

"I was feeding grain one night. Early December, I think. Bitter cold, must have been about 10 degrees out. Snowing just a bit, like tonight. You know, when the sheep hear the sound of the grain hitting the feeders, they all rush in for it."

Owen nodded. He had almost been knocked down a couple times himself while doing this. His grandfather continued.

"Well, they were all eating, but I didn't see my big ram. He was a white-faced one—a Dorset. He's usually the first one there, he pushes the others out of the way," Grandpa Elmer said.

Owen leaned forward, listening intently.

"I had my old 30-30 Winchester in the barn after I started losing a few, so I grabbed that and headed down into the pasture." The older man paused and looked into the fire for a moment, then raised his glance back to Owen and continued.

"Well, it was just about dark...I don't know, maybe it only comes out when the sun starts to go down. Anyways, I just got down to the edge of the woods, and I guess I saw pretty much the same thing that you did. I think I was further off, though—I don't think I ever got closer than thirty yards or so. I saw it just as it was going into the woods, but I could see it carrying the ram," he said.

"Did you shoot at it?" Owen asked.

"No, I didn't. I didn't know what it was, walking on two legs like that," Owen's grandfather said, tamping down a small pinch of tobacco into his pipe. "Didn't want to wake up the next morning and find out I'd shot a man. But I guess I knew it wasn't a man...even at the time."

"Did you tell anybody?" Owen asked, his eyes wide at this revelation.

"I told my brother Dan. I didn't think anyone else would believe me. He came over the next couple nights and we waited out there with shotguns, but it never showed up again. I showed him some of the footprints, and he believed me." He paused in silence for a moment. "Dan went off to the war in France a couple months after that. Got killed at Belleau Wood. I never told your grandmother about what I saw—in fact I never told another soul about it...until now," he said, drawing on his pipe. He leaned forward and put another small log onto the fire.

Owen looked back into the flames, his eyes unfocused, as he tried to take in the story.

"I remember when I was a little tyke, no more than six or seven," Grandpa Elmer continued. "This old man in town, Joe Crow they called him—they said he was part Indian, but my pa said he wasn't— used to tell all kinds of wild stories. They said he was in the Union army during the Civil War, and after Chancellorsville was never quite the same. Anyways, I think he told a story about this thing once. People would get him drinking and telling stories, just so they could laugh at him. I remember once I was down at the general store with my pa, and he started telling about some thing he saw in the fields the night before, that walked on two legs but wasn't a man. I remember my pa telling him not to scare a child, and he got me out of there. I think that's what he was talking about. Or I don't know, maybe I just got that in my head after I saw it."

Owen opened his mouth and leaned forward to speak, but no words came out.

"Well, you just try to get all your chores done early from now on, and stay close to the barn once it starts to get dark," the older man said. "I'll put up some more fence tomorrow, and we'll keep the sheep in that first pasture for the next couple of weeks. I'll give them the grain in the afternoon...you'll just have to feed them the hay, and make sure they've got clean water. You can do that right after school—how does that sound?"

Owen nodded blankly.

"I was mighty uneasy going down there for the next couple of weeks after I saw it, mighty uneasy, I'm sure. Can't just stay in the house scared, though. Things got to be done," Grandpa Elmer said, with an air of resolution. "I don't think it'll be back anytime soon."

"Come on men, dinner's ready!" Owen's mother yelled from the kitchen.

Owen's grandfather winced slightly as he shifted his weight to get out of the chair, and he had that familiar glint in his eyes that he always got when he was told a meal was ready.

Owen had a small tempest of questions and concerns churning away inside him, but he also knew that his grandfather wasn't hiding anything from him.

"Sometimes even us old folks don't have all the answers, Owen, and some things are best not talked about too much," the older man said. Owen felt Grandpa Elmer's gentle but firm hand on his shoulder, and they walked together to the kitchen.

A Girl in Trouble

Captain Jini Wong shielded her eyes against the sun and looked up at the two giant scavenger bats that were circling high above her. *You haven't got yourselves a meal just yet.* If she still had her flash rifle she might have taken a shot at them, even though the noise could draw unwanted attention. She had been walking for two days across the blue sands and scrub brush of the Great Northern Desert of Yu-tab, and she had at least another two to go before she reached the nearest Union of Greater Earth outpost—and not two Earth days, either, but 31 hour Yu-tab days. When hours might mean the difference between life and death, this fact was not negligible.

The plasma rocket attack on her jump-hover couldn't have been a direct hit; it had knocked her unconscious and overboard into the sand, but the vehicle and her crew kept going. At least she figured that was probably what had happened, since there was nothing and nobody in sight when she regained consciousness. Her comlink was smashed, her weapon was nowhere to be found, and the only food she had was the emergency N-ration tubes that were built into her daysuit. Water, though—that was no problem. Three flexpacks had fallen off the transport; they were probably the ones that she and Leito had hung on the side rail for easy access. That would last her for a good while, and she had just eaten shortly before the attack, so food wasn't an immediate concern. She figured it was better to start making time immediately, before hunger and fatigue inevitably began to take their toll. She gathered what she could and started walking west, towards the outpost. After an hour or two, when the jump-hover failed to show, she figured that the rest of her squad was either dead, or walking like she was. Had they been mobile, her crew would have circled the craft back for her already. There weren't many other likely scenarios; the Jurona didn't take prisoners.

And so she had started walking, and now, two days later, she was still walking. The cut on her forehead had scabbed over, and although her left shoulder was still sore, she didn't think it was anything serious. All things considered, it could have been much worse.

It was nearly midday, but at this time of year the temperature didn't fluctuate much between day and night in the Great Northern Desert. Still, as she plodded along through the endless blue sands, she began to feel the toll that both the crash and the desert had taken on her. No rescue party had been sent out for her from the UGE outpost, apparently. Maybe her crew wasn't able to send out a distress signal in time. Her craft, like most of the jump-hovers they used, was just a retrofitted native Yu-tabi vehicle, and wasn't equipped with any tracking devices. And the receivers and reflector wave sensors that the UGE employed at their bases didn't always seem to work that well in the Yu-tabi atmosphere. Then again, it was also possible that the UGE command had indeed monitored the attack, and had just written her off as being lost with the rest of the crew. The reasons weren't all that important. She was on her own.

She scanned the horizon. Without her electroview, her range was limited to what she could see with the naked eye during daylight hours. There was nothing but the sands, scrub brush, and the occasional outcropping of rocks and boulders behind her and to either side. The blue-gold landscape gently but steadily sloped up to a ridge about twenty kilometers ahead of her. Once she got to the top of that, it would be an easy, if long, downhill hike from there to the UGE outpost.

She heard that faint barking sound from high above. She glanced up, and saw that the scavenger bats were still floating and circling in their standard pattern. They had their eyes on her—that she knew with certainty.

"Oh, you're hungry," she said. "Join the crowd. And besides, you really wouldn't get much of a meal from me. I'd be hardly more than a couple bites for you." She pulled one of the flexpacks of water off her shoulder, pushed aside the undershirt that she was using as a headdress, and took a long drink. This flexpack was about a third full, and she still had another one that hadn't been opened. She had one N-ration tube left, as well. As long as she stayed on track, that should last until she got to the outpost.

She looked back up to the single sun of Yu-tab and its relation to its moon to check her direction, and continued on. She would be more than happy and relieved to get to the base. She knew almost everyone there quite well—and really, all the UGE forces on Yu-tab were a fairly close-knit group. Most of the troopers signed up for five-year hitches, and once you got there, there really wasn't anyplace to go. She was on her third year, although she was still thought of as the "new girl". For the most part, they all knew what they were getting into, and they took pride in their unit and in their assigned roles. They were a motley crew, but Jini Wong liked most of them. Jackson was her favorite. He wasn't much to look at, with his paunch, patchy red hair and mean-looking face; he was nearing retirement and didn't suffer fools gladly, but he was genuinely kind and had a wicked sense of humor. He was an unlisted soldier, and he had always shown Jini the proper respect due her rank—but she gradually came to see that he didn't exactly relate to other officers in that way. She guessed that Jackson's respect for her was more personal than professional, and that was fine with her. She smiled as she remembered the time Quadrant Inspector Fleming visited Yu-tab. As he toured the base, he noticed Jackson kicking back on a chair. "Trooper, haven't you got anything to do?" he asked, at which point Jackson jumped up and said "Yes sir. I certainly do, sir," and then he got down on his knees with his handkerchief and attempted to shine the inspector's boots. The inspector frowned, and as he walked away slightly confused, Jackson bowed several times in mock subservience. He then shot Jini a quick wink and grin. Jini smiled at the memory.

"Jackson, I could use some of your laughs right about now," she said out loud. She walked along through the drifting sands for another hour, and then found herself passing through a small patch of orange-horned scrub brush. She stopped. She cocked her head, and then heard it.

The creaky rattling of a Juronan wind-horse.

Her heart began beating faster, and she put her hand to her brow as she scanned the horizon. There, far in the distance in the direction she had come from, she could just make them out. Two. Coming after her.

She broke into a jog, measured but steady. Being on the short and stocky side, she preferred sprints to long distance running, but she was as fit as she had ever been—and the prospect of being taken by the Jurona was as much motivation as any human could need. If she was captured, a slow, painful death was the most likely outcome—and not necessarily the worst possible one. Command said that rumors of the Jurona eating human prisoners could not be confirmed, but she knew a couple troopers who said it was so, and these men knew the Great Northern Desert as well as anyone.

The Juronan wind-horses were strange vehicles. No engines, no wheels—just a contraption of multiple wooden legs, levers, and pulleys, powered by sail. No human (and no Yu-tabi, for that matter) had ever managed to ride a captured one for more than a meter or two before it collapsed into a broken tangle of sticks, strings and sails. The Jurona started on them in their youth, it was said, and by the time they were adults, riding them came as natural as walking. They actually preferred them to power vehicles for scouting and patrols on the planets they invaded, even though they had technologically superior options. Some in UGE command speculated that there was some religious or philosophical symbolism to them, but nobody seemed to know the details on that. On Yu-tab, they had apparently been modified with modern deflectors and weaponry, and if there was a good wind blowing the wind-horses could reach remarkable speeds. Unfortunately for Jini Wong, there was a good wind blowing today.

She kept up her steady jog, and looked back over her shoulder. The two wind-horses were still probably a half hour away, but the time-frame was not that important. It didn't even matter if they had spotted her or not—although they most likely had. They certainly couldn't miss her trail. And she couldn't outrun them.

She saw a large slab of red rock up ahead, jutting out of the blue sand like a stalagmite. It was ringed by more of the orange-horned brush, and there was even a tiny bit of shade from a large green Denbo weed that grew close to the rock. She slowed to a walk as she came into the semi-oasis, and she sat down in the shade to assess her situation. She pulled both flexpacks off her back, and drank the one empty. If she was going to die out here in the desert anyway, there was no reason to die thirsty. She leaned back against the rock and wiped the sweat and sand from her brow with her headdress. The sands of Yu-tab had the strangest scent, almost like a subtle spice, and she liked the smell of that and her sweat together after a long day on patrol. It was the scent of life and nature, and of her doing her day's work as a part of something bigger than herself. That today might be her last day alive didn't frighten her, but it did bring to mind some regrets and wistful memories. She thought briefly of her childhood, and walking with her parents and brother through the calm, peaceful forest in Wulingyuan National Park back on Earth, on a cool spring day. She could still remember the scents of the pines and the tittering of the songbirds. She thought of her freshman year at the UGE Academy on Mars. A year later she had a boyfriend, and they had made love, and she thought it so strange that her first time wasn't on Earth—something that would have been impossible to even imagine for her ancestors.

"No," she said out loud. *She wasn't dead yet.* If, when the moment came, her life was going to flash before her eyes anyway, she didn't need to help it along. She took a deep, slow breath and closed her eyes. She brought her palms up to her forehead and rubbed them down her cheeks and jaw. *Think.* She took off the jacket of her daysuit and checked the pockets, even though she already knew exactly what was in them. There was still the large N-ration tube, and she took it out. She opened the top and squeezed out a small mouthful. She was so hungry and it tasted so good, she almost squeezed the rest into her mouth. But she stopped. She closed the tube back up and put it back in its webbing, and then she reached into a tiny pocket hidden in the back of the jacket and pulled out a small black plastic box. She opened it up, and saw the single blue suicide capsule, filled with its dose of deadly powder. She closed the box. It was something to consider.

She had pretty much decided on her plan when she heard the creaking and flapping of the wind-horses as they came nearer to her makeshift camp. She glanced out from behind the rock, and despite her palpable fear, she marveled at the sight of the two wind-horses in full operation; they were a strange marvel of engineering and a perfect symphony of coordination between pilot, craft and wind. Then she noticed something else. There was a Ji-lizard striding out in front, tethered to the second wind-horse on a long cord. The Jurona used the Ji-lizards like scent-hounds on Earth, although they certainly had none of the charm of dogs. They walked on four legs and were about two meters long and a meter high, with rows of razor-sharp teeth and a disposition to match. They came from Jurona, and they were apparently especially well-adapted to life on Yu-tab. It was said that they liked the taste of men, as well. She looked back up at the scavenger bats circling overhead. *Was there anything out here that didn't want to eat you?*

Jini scanned her immediate surrounding again. The weeds and brush provided nothing long or stiff enough to be used as a spear or staff. She bent down and picked up a rock with a sharp point. So this is what it had come to, she thought—a stone-age weapon against the Juronan scouts who were armed with their latest flash rifles.

The Ji-lizard turned, and its tongue flicked out. It hissed, and turned towards the rock Jini was hiding behind. Jini gripped her stone weapon tightly and pressed her back up against the rock, ready to smash whatever came around to challenge her.

Then she heard the guttural clicking of the Juronans for the first time—for the first time in her life, actually. She had seen the videos and gone through the training, but this was different. It was real life. The sound was partly simian, partly avian. She carefully peered around the rock, exposing as little of her head as possible. She saw the Ji-lizard staring right back at her, no more than ten meters away. Its black eyes focused directly on her and its foot-long red tongue flicked out again, tasting her scent. Behind them she got her first view of the Juronans. She didn't particularly like the term, but with one look she instinctively understood why many of her fellow troopers referred to the Jurona as "Cycs." They were bipedal, and about the same height as men—although much heavier and more broad-chested. Their whole body was covered in a thick brown hair, but that wasn't the distinguishing feature. Their one eye, in the center of their forehead, was.

"Come...out," the first Juronan said, in passable English. "Or we...send dog in." Jini saw the Ji-lizard strain at its tether, and she had no doubt that if it was released, it would be on her in the blink of an eye. She came out from behind the rock, holding her gear sack. She raised both hands up in the air, and slowly walked out as she and the Ji-lizard warily eyed each other.

"Throw down...things," one of the Juronans said from astride his wind-horse. Both he and his companion had their flash weapons trained on her. She did as she was told.

The Juronans both dismounted their vehicles, and Jini Wong still couldn't figure out exactly how they did it. They seemed to effortlessly climb down between a maze of sticks and pulleys, and as they came off the vehicles the wind-horses collapsed to almost half their previous size, and into an apparently patternless jumble of their constituent parts. The Ji-lizard was still tethered to the one wind-horse. The two Juronans walked up to her, one in front and the other following, their weapons held at the ready. They had an odd simian gait, and Jini could feel her heart pounding as they approached. One of them stopped about two meters in front of her and aimed his weapon at her head, its one eye staring at her, unblinking. The other walked around her and went back behind the rock where she had been hiding. It came out a moment later, not finding anything.

"Are you from ship?" The one aiming its weapon at her asked. She didn't answer.

"We track you. You are from ship. We destroy ship and kill all."

Jini felt a sharp pang of grief and anger, but she didn't show any expression. The other Juronan said something in its own language, and it walked back around in front of Jini. It came up close to her and looked her in the eye. It was so close she could smell its strange scent. In one quick motion it swung its long arm and hit Jini on the side of the face with its leathery hand. It was as hard as Jini had ever been struck in her life, and she dropped instantly.

She didn't think she lost consciousness, but if she had, it was only for a few seconds. She could taste blood flowing from her nose as she leaned up on her elbow.

The one that had struck her was going through her gear, and the one with its weapon trained on her spoke. "Female...human, maybe if you have food rations for us, we won't eat you."

Whether that was a dark joke or a statement of fact, Jini wasn't sure. If these Juronans were capable of humor, she had not seen either of them smile.

The Jurona required water like humans, although it was said they could go much longer without drinking. The one picked up her flexpack and slid the cap off. It sniffed, and then took a small drink. It threw the pack to the other one, who caught it and took a similar swallow. They both had re-slung their weapons over their shoulders, and now seemed unconcerned with Jini.

The one continued rifling through her pack, and pulled out the N-ration tube. It opened the top and squeezed out a small bit of the concentrate, and tentatively tasted it. It grunted its approval and then squeezed out a much larger portion, and ate that. The other Jurona said something in a demanding tone, and the first took another quick swallow of the paste and then threw the tube to its companion.

The other Juronan smelled the paste, and squeezed some into its mouth. It chewed slowly, and swallowed.

“Food is good. You, go,” the Juronan said, not looking at her as it sucked to get every last bit from the tube. “You will run, we give you time before we follow. Maybe you will get free, if you run fast.”

Jini got to her knees and then stood up. She looked at the flexpack of water in the sand, still mostly full, and she looked back at the Juronan.

“Go now. Or we will kill you here. You will take nothing. You will run,” it said.

Jini turned and walked quickly for several steps, and then she broke into a run. She headed in the direction she had been going before, up towards the ridge. She ran for several minutes, looking around in all directions for some natural shelter where she could possibly hide, or at least make a stand, but there was nothing. Nothing but the drifting sands and the odd rock and shrub. She knew the Jurona didn’t allow captured prisoners to live; they certainly wouldn’t let her go free. They were just having their sport with her, and there was no way she could outrun them. She figured that she had made the wrong decision regarding the suicide pill, and now her end would most likely be violent and not particularly quick.

She alternated running and jogging for almost half an hour, and then finally had to stop to catch her breath. She put her hands on her knees and bent over, gasping for air. She turned around, expecting to see the wind-horses coming after her, but she saw nothing. She had a fairly good view of the oasis where the Jurona had captured her, but all she could see were vague shapes and the formation of rocks and shrubs. She couldn't detect any movement. Other than a light wind blowing through, there was no sound. Not even the barking of those damned bats. *The scavenger bats.* She looked up, but they weren't there. They had been tracking her constantly from when she had first started walking right up until the Juronans caught her. *Was it possible...?*

She thought about her options. She was exhausted and had no food or water, and even if they didn't come after her, she would die from exposure before she ever made it back to the base. She turned and started walking back towards the Juronans. About forty-five minutes later, she came back to the oasis and the familiar setting of their makeshift camp.

The Juronans were both dead, lying about five meters apart, and each had one of the giant scavenger bats perched on it. The one Juronan was face-down, and the bat had eaten away most of its back and legs. The other was lying on its back, and its head was completely gone as the bat gnawed on the Juronan's neck and shoulder.

"Get away!" Jini shouted, as she waved her arms and walked up towards them. One of the great black bats barked at her, but they both flapped and flew up into the air several meters; they were easily frightened away by any prey that might still fight back. The two bats landed side by side on one of the collapsed wind-horses and watched her. The Ji-lizard was still tethered to the other wind-horse, and it alternately hissed at both Jini and the bats, unable to reach any of them.

Jini walked over and retrieved her flexpack from the sand, and brought it to her mouth. It was still mostly full and she took a drink of the tepid water. Not too big a drink though, as she'd need to ration it if she was going to make it back to the post. Food, though—that was going to be an issue.

She reached down and picked up the flash rifle that had fallen where one of the Juronans had dropped it. The Ji-lizard was still angry and hissing as it strained against its leash to reach her. The two bats teetered restlessly on the wind-horse, intently eying both their carrion and her. Captain Jini Wong looked the rifle over—it was alien and a little strange, but it didn't take her long to figure out which way to point it.

"I realize that we're all hungry here," Jini said wearily, "and I hate to break this to you—but only one of us is going to have dinner." She brought the flash rifle up to her shoulder and fired, and with a strange whine the blue beam sliced through the two bats, killing them instantly.

"Your turn," she said as she turned to the hissing Ji-lizard, and the beam she fired virtually bisected the creature lengthwise.

***

She had taken a big chance by emptying the powder from her suicide capsule into the N-ration tube instead of ingesting it herself. In the first place, she couldn't be sure that the Juronans would eat it—and even then, she wasn't sure it would kill them. Apparently it took a little longer for it to work on them than it would have on a human, but her gamble had paid off.

She was just finishing the last bites of the Ji-lizard steak she had roasted when she heard the faint whirring of an approaching craft. As it got closer, she recognized the sound of a small Yu-tabi jump-hover. She stood up and saw it coming in from the south-west. It was UGE, and there was a man standing on the bow. It was Jackson.

"I'll be damned," Jackson shouted, as he jumped off the hover before it had completely stopped. As he walked over to Jini, he looked around at evidence of the struggle. "I knew you were kinda tough, but I wouldn't have guessed you had *this* in you. I figured if you were still alive out here, you'd be in a whole mess of trouble. Not sittin' down to Sunday dinner."

Jini walked up to him, and Jackson saluted. Captain Wong returned the salute, paused for a moment, and then fell into Jackson's arms as the two embraced. They were a study in contrasts, with tall, broad-chested Jackson in his clean, crisp blue-gray trooper uniform, and short, compact Jini in the dirty, blood-stained remains of her own.

"Come on, we've got to go," said the pilot. "We've already been gone too long, and we're losing daylight fast. And with no crew, I don't want to tangle with any Juronan patrols. It'll be my ass if this goes wrong."

Jini raised an eyebrow at Jackson.

"Yeah, this mission wasn't exactly authorized by command. I was barely able to talk Voss here into piloting us. But I don't think we'll get in too much trouble for bringin' you back safe and sound."

She and Jackson climbed aboard the jump-hover, and in a moment they were on their way back to the base. Jackson and Voss wanted to hear her story, and she would want to tell it. But not now. The three rode in silence over the blue sands of the Great Northern Desert as the sun set on Yu-tab.

The Lighthouse

The wind had picked up quite dramatically over the last half hour as the three men made their way steadily along the narrow cobblestone street. The rain began to come as well, and being propelled by the strong gale, it hit the men with a stinging force. The tall man in the lead turned up the collar of his long oilskin coat, and he pulled his hat down as he turned his head away from the driving wind. The three continued on without a word. The main street they were walking on was relatively deserted, even though it was a Saturday night. By mid-November in Charlesport, however, this wasn't unusual. The streets were often quite empty at this time of year, as the summer tourist flood had long since receded and the fishing season was off its peak. The three walked by a few darkened buildings and then came up to the door of "The Red Rooster", the tavern's wooden sign swinging and banging fiercely in the wind. The light from the windows and the music and conversation seeping out from within were a welcome contrast to the inclement weather, and the tall man opened the door and held it as the other two went in ahead of him.

As the door closed behind them, the three relaxed slightly and they began taking off their hats, gloves, and coats. The warmth emanating from the big fireplace, and the aroma of ale, pipe tobacco and simmering chowder from the small kitchen soothed their senses.

"Who's that? Jack, William...and Reverend Morgan?" said the

barmaid, smiling, as she walked by with a tray holding several pints of ale. "Reverend, aren't you a naughty one? Here it is half-past eleven on a Saturday, when you have to work tomorrow!"

"Oh, I'll be taking it easy tonight, Katherine," said Reverend Morgan. "And you can call me Daniel outside of the office." He said this with a smile, but there was little trace of humor in his tone. The Reverend was a short man, with a medium build and a rather thick shock of dusty blonde hair. Although he was forty-five, he could have easily passed for ten years younger.

"All right then," Katherine said, hiding her smile, "but I'll be keeping my eye on you three. Did you boys want to sit at the bar?"

The bar was over to the left and had a number of younger men and women there, obviously in good spirits, and they were engaged in animated laughter and conversation. Just to the other side of the bar was a young fiddler and an older guitar player, and the duo was playing some slow Irish airs.

"I don't think so," Jack Hayes said. "We'll just take that table over in the back corner." The barmaid smiled and nodded.

Jack was tall and thin, and a few months over forty-six. His black hair already was mixed with more than a few gray ones, and his face had the strong, weather-worn look that one would expect of someone who made their living out at sea, which Jack did. He led the way over to the corner table, and the other two followed him. They sat down, weary from a trying day, but without the familiar satisfaction of a normal day's effort behind them. The three of them sat there for a couple of minutes with no words spoken, and each with an unfocused, blank stare at nothing in particular.

"What can I get you?" asked the barmaid, as she came back to their table.

“Three whiskeys and three porters, if you please, dear,” said William Stanton in his deep, resonant voice. He was one of those men who seemed to be able to speak strongly and forcefully with very little effort and at a very low volume. Stanton was a stout man of average height, a few years past forty, and although his dark brown hair was thinning on top, it was countered by his thick mutton-chop sideburns. “You can put them on my tab, Katherine.”

“Be right back with them, Mr. Stanton,” the barmaid said cheerfully, as she went to fill the order.

Stanton leaned back in his chair and then put his hand to his breast pocket, his brow furrowed. He felt the familiar shape, twitched a half smile, and then reached his hand in to pull out his pipe and tobacco pouch. The others remained silent as Stanton went through the familiar motions of putting the tobacco in the bowl and tamping it down. He lit it and drew in the smoke, and the glow from the match subtly lit up his face. In his countenance his two companions saw a reflection of their own somber moods. The barmaid returned with a tray of three pints and three shots, and she set one pair down in front of each man. Stanton smiled and thanked her, and he leaned back and took another draw on his pipe. Jack Hayes leaned forward and took a drink of ale, but Reverend Morgan just absentmindedly ran his finger along the rim of the whiskey glass.

“Had to be done, you know,” Stanton said. “Can hardly believe it myself. And truth be told I *wouldn’t* believe it if I hadn’t been there. Damnedest thing I ever saw. I’ll say it clear: you two were right.”

“I wish to God we hadn’t been,” Hayes said, taking another long drink of his ale.

"Did it really happen?" The Reverend asked, lifting his glass and looking at it a moment before taking a sip.

"It happened," Jack Hayes said.

***

Five hours ago, none of them had quite fathomed the extent of what was to take place that night. It was a typical mid-November evening in the seaside Massachusetts town of Charlesport, some thirty miles north of Boston. It was already quite dark at a little after six in the evening, and the air was damp and clammy, making the wind seem a good deal colder than the thermometer's forty-three degrees. The three of them had agreed to meet on one of the side docks off the main pier, where Jack Hayes had his dinghy tied up. Most of the lobster boats had already come in for the evening, and there wasn't much activity on the pier in general, but they still wanted to keep away from any prying eyes. Jack was already there, loading some gear into the dinghy, and as the two dark silhouettes walked silently toward him, he recognized his old friends William Stanton and the Reverend Daniel Morgan.

"William, Dan. You made it all right," Jack said, tossing a couple of life preservers into the small boat.

"You think we're going to need those, Jack?" the Reverend said.

"Nah, the sea's not too rough out there tonight. This wind ain't more'n twenty knots. Not enough to give us any trouble. I just thought I'd put 'em in there to give you landlubbers some peace of mind."

“Peace of mind is one thing I don’t have about this,” Stanton said in his deep voice. He coughed a couple times and cleared his throat. He looked out at the water and squinted into the wind. “This isn’t a night to be out in, if I had anything to say about it.”

“You can say anything you want, William,” Jack said, with a hint of challenge. “Nobody’s forcing you to go. You don’t have to be a part of this if you don’t want to.”

“I’ve got a good mind to take you up on that, you know,” Stanton said. “Craziest thing I’ve ever heard, really now! If it was anyone else but you two told me that, I’d have thrown you out of my office right into the street! And called the nuthouse while I was at it!”

“But it wasn’t anyone else,” the Reverend said. “It was only the two of us.”

“And that’s the real catch, isn’t it? And that’s why I’m here,” Stanton said, with a tone of resignation. “Friendship,” he added, “is a highly dubious justification for *anything*, as far as I’m concerned. There’s a reason it’s not a valid defense in a court of law.”

The Reverend smiled. “Oh, I know there’s more to you than a lawyer, William.”

“And I would hope there’s more to you two than superstitious simpletons, but I may be mistaken,” Stanton said.

“Nothing make-believe about the bodies found,” Hayes said without looking up, as he untied the small boat from the mooring. “All dry of blood.”

“There were exactly three bodies found,” Stanton said. “It’s true the coroner had trouble fixing the cause of death, but they had been in the water a considerable period of time. It doesn’t prove anything—least of all what you two are suggesting."

"It weren't only three that was found," Jack said. "It was only three that was picked up."

"More bodies were found?" Stanton asked, thrown off his argument a bit.

"A lot of men here out on the boats wouldn't touch any more after they found the first few. Said the bodies weren't natural. There was another three or four out there the last few weeks."

"Ah, yes," Stanton said. "The testimony of superstitious fisherman. That's certainly a logical, convincing bit of evidence. Were there any sea serpents seen as well?"

Jack Hayes smiled as he stood up. "Look, William. I won't try to tell you the law, and you don't tell me what happens or doesn't happen out to sea—because we'd both be talking out of our asses. Agreed?"

"Have it your way," Stanton said, smiling. "And tomorrow I'll be having a good laugh at your expense."

"At any rate I don't think it's anything to laugh about," Reverend Morgan said, "either now or tomorrow. But anyways, we're just going to talk to him tonight, and then we'll know for sure."

"Aye, we can talk," Jack said. "But you'd best be prepared for more than talking—the both of you. This ain't fun and games."

Stanton rolled his eyes. "I *am* prepared for more. I'm prepared to laugh heartily at your expense on the way back."

Reverend Morgan shook his head. "I want you both to remember that Edmund is our friend, and has been our friend for many years. It's his best interest that should concern us, above all else."

"Well then, let's get going," Stanton said. "Oh heavens," he said in his booming voice as he looked down into the dinghy, "I'm not going to be expected to row this thing, am I?"

***

The three of them got into the dinghy. Jack took his place behind the oars, and they set out from the pier. The night was overcast, and the moon appeared from behind the clouds only intermittently. The waves were no more than a foot high, and Jack Hayes was quite calm and methodical in his rowing. Still, Stanton and Reverend Morgan weren't all that comfortable.

"How can you see where you're going?" Stanton asked. "Why don't we light the lantern?"

"No, we don't want to call attention to ourselves," the Reverend said. "We're only a couple hundred feet from shore, anyways. See those lights back there, William? That's the town of Charlesport, where we just came from."

"Very funny," Stanton said. "I wasn't worried about getting lost, I was worried about us running into something."

"What are we going to run into? We're in the middle of the bay." the Reverend replied.

"Keep it down you two, if you don't want to draw attention. Voices carry over the water at night," Jack said, as he kept up his rowing. "William, we're just going to stay close to shore until we come around to the channel between the mainland and Shepherd's Island. From the channel we'll be able to see the light from Ten Cask."

Ten Cask Island was just about a mile and a half off the coast of Charlesport, and its lighthouse warned ships of the dangerous shoals surrounding it. It was not a large island, no more than a mile long and three-quarters of a mile at its widest; in total it consisted of about fifty acres. In the summer it attracted naturalists and sightseers, with one scenic trail around the edge of the island and several more intersecting inland. Residents of Charlesport and the surrounding towns, and sometimes summer tourists up from Boston, would sail out to the island and moor their boats just offshore and then take a dinghy to the single landing and enjoy an afternoon of sightseeing and picnicking. On the rocky eastern side of the island were the many nests of the Herring gulls and the Great Black-backed gulls, which were quite active and noisy during the summer, as the spring chicks hatched and the parents met any interlopers who got too close to the nests with an angry vocal challenge.

The most striking feature of the island, however, was the lighthouse. It had the distinction of being the last one built by the British in North America, just before revolution and war created the new country. It stood some one hundred and seventy feet tall, firmly sitting on a granite ledge on the north side, and its gray stones bore the weathering of many years of salt air and ocean winds. From the catwalk at the top one could see the Boston skyline, some thirty miles to the southwest, and on a clear day one could look to the northwest and make out the peak of Mount Agamenticus on the coast of Maine.

After Labor Day, as the flow of summer visitors turned to a

trickle, the atmosphere of the island began to change. The subtle chill, even during the sunny daylight hours, made one forget the balmy days of August and think instead of the colder months to come. The surrounding ocean, which only a few short weeks ago was refreshingly cool, was slowly transforming into the dangerous, merciless sea that it always was in the winter.

There were no permanent residents on the island during the winter, save the lighthouse keeper, and his family, if he had one. Over the years, there had been several keepers in the house, and the last one, Jacob Alfredson, had lived there year-round with his wife and three children. He had taken the job when he was in his early twenties, and he and his wife had raised their family there and stayed on after the children had grown and left. Only last year, in 1904, had Jacob's health begun failing, and his wife felt that they couldn't be alone on the island for another winter. They had moved into a small cottage in town near their daughter's family not long after that. That was when the town accepted the application of Edmund Hodge as keeper. That was when the trouble began.

***

With Jack's steady rowing, the trio made their way across the bay. The sea was very calm so far, although Jack had told them that the wind and the waves would be picking up later, if the weather forecasts were correct.

"Say, that's the Dalton house up ahead, I believe," Stanton half-whispered to his companions, as he pointed to a house on the shore. "I was at a party there this past July 4th, beautiful view over the water from that patio."

"We're coming up to the channel," Jack said quietly. "Should be able to see the lighthouse as we get around the corner."

The Dalton house sat up on the rocks right at the tip of the mainland, directly across the channel from Shepherd's Island. The channel itself was quite narrow, only two hundred yards or so, and as Jack continued rowing they passed around the tip of the mainland and into the gap.

"There she is," Jack said, as the beam from the Ten Cask Island lighthouse circled around on its endless rotation. The water was a bit rougher in the channel than it was in the bay by the mainland, but it still wasn't too choppy.

"For the life of me, I still can't imagine Edmund taking this job," Stanton said. "I mean, you two have known him as long as I have. Is there anyone you'd imagine who'd be *less* likely to spend a winter by himself in a dreary lighthouse? Now Jack here, sure—I'm almost surprised he never took the position. But Edmund? I just don't see it."

"Mmm. He was always a talker, that one. Liked the ladies, liked the parties, liked being out and about, I guess you'd say," Jack said, his voice still kept low. "Something about that time in Europe, I'd say. Studying, he was. Studying what, I'm not too sure. Made a lot of odd friends, and got a lot of queer ideas in his head, if you ask me."

"Eh, I've spent some time on the Continent myself, and met a lot of fine folks. Nothing wrong with the universities over there. Travel opens the mind," Stanton said.

"Depends on what your mind is opened to, I reckon," Reverend

Morgan said. "I think Jack's right. Edmund was never quite the same after he came back last spring. I stopped by once in early June to see him. Had some of his friends from overseas there with him—they were a strange lot. Don't know exactly where they were from...Belgium, Holland? A handsome young blonde couple and an older man. Not friendly at all, and Edmund seemed rather uncomfortable that I should meet them."

As Jack kept rowing steadily, they made their way through the narrow channel and out into the open ocean. The island was less than a mile away, but both Stanton and the Reverend felt a little uneasy at being out of the protected harbor. Stanton looked down into the impenetrable, dark water.

"Sharks down there, I suppose," he said.

"Sharks are in the ocean, that's indeed a fact," Jack said.

"But, are there sharks around *here*, is what I mean."

"Sharks are in the ocean," Jack said with a laugh. "That's about as specific as I can get for you. I've never heard of a shark leapin' out of the water and swallowin' a dinghy with three men on it, if that'll make you feel better."

"Yes, I suppose it does," Stanton decided.

"No sir," Jack said, pausing for effect. "There was only two in that dinghy back in aught-two."

"Please, we need to be serious here," Reverend Morgan said.

"Now take it easy, Dan," Jack said, "I'm just tryin' to lighten the mood a bit."

"I know. I'm sorry, Jack," the Reverend said. "I'm a bit edgy."

No one said anything for a few minutes, as they continued rowing out to the island. The wind had picked up, and as the beam from the lighthouse made its circuit, the briefly illuminated waves were starting to crest a bit higher.

"I must say I really don't like this," Stanton said, as the boat began to rise and fall more noticeably. The bow of the boat came down a bit hard off from one wave, and splashed some water into the boat. Stanton brushed some drops off the shoulder of his oilskin coat and grumbled again.

"Sometimes things got to be done," Jack said. "He's our friend, William. Can't just abandon him to...God knows what."

"And that's fine," Stanton said. "If he's got some problems with strong drink, or something not right in the old noggin—hey, it happens to the best of men. But when you start bringing up this religious mumbo-jumbo—no offense, Daniel—then you start to lose me. Why in blazes do we have to go out here in the middle of the night?"

"So we can talk to him, that's why," the Reverend said.

"Why couldn't we talk to him during the day?"

"Well, that's something we'll have to ask him," Jack said. "Cause when he sent that letter to Dan, he told us to only come see him at night. Ain't that right, Dan?"

"That's what he said, and he was very specific. Said his nerves were bad and that he had to sleep during the day— and under no circumstances should we visit during the daylight hours."

"He told that to Fitch Harper, too. Fitch goes out to the island every couple weeks with supplies and mail and what-not. He told Fitch to just leave the stuff by the landing, and he'd pick it up at night," Jack continued. "It ain't natural."

"Hogwash," Stanton said haughtily. "I'm sure being out here all by yourself with no one to talk to all day would make anyone a little odd. When someone doesn't live a normal life, is it a surprise that they don't keep a normal schedule? And besides, if you're a lighthouse keeper, aren't your most important duties at night? Seems to make sense to me."

"Well, that may be so," Jack said, as he exchanged a quick glance with the Reverend. "That may be so."

"We're getting close," Reverend Morgan said, pointing forward. "I think I can make out the landing." The wind was stronger now, and a bit of a misty rain was starting to come down. A couple hundred yards ahead lay the island, and the sound of waves breaking on its seaward shore became louder as the three men approached.

Stanton brought his right hand up to shield his eyes from the misty rain, leaned past Jack, and peered ahead. "Yes, there it is." He could make out the dock, just below a small boathouse. The immense gray tower of the lighthouse rose up behind it. "Are we just going to land there, or approach from another side?"

"We're not sneaking up on him. We're just going to land like anyone else would," Jack said.

"Remember, William," the Reverend added, "we have a standing invitation, of sorts, and we're just here to talk to him."

"And besides, unless you fancy climbing up the outside of the lighthouse, we need him to open the door and let us in, "Jack said.

"All right, fine with me," Stanton said. "We'll go in the front door, right as rain."

Jack Hayes continued rowing, and the three passed the remaining distance in silence. The rain was turning from a fine mist into more of a steady downfall, although it still wasn't very heavy. Jack brought the dinghy in until it bumped the edge of the dock, and the Reverend steadied himself and climbed out of the boat. Jack threw him the rope and Reverend Morgan secured the dinghy as Jack and Stanton climbed out. Jack examined the knot the Reverend had used to tie the boat up.

"Hey, that's not bad for a landlubber," he said.

"There were a few fishermen on my mother's side, you know," Reverend Morgan said.

The three of them made their way to the end of the dock and up the stone steps to the boathouse. Jack and the Reverend were both carrying small canvas satchels over their backs, and Jack set his on the ground. He reached in and brought out a small kerosene lamp. He lit it quickly, stood up and swung his satchel over his back. The light from the lamp didn't carry very far in the starless, rainy night, but the small glow it did have cut through the gloom sufficiently so that the three could at least see a couple yards ahead of them.

"Have you been on the island recently, Jack?" Stanton asked.

"Not much since I was a boy," Jack Hayes responded. "I was pals with the Alfredson kids when he was the keeper, and I visited them quite often. But I've probably only set foot here a couple of times in the last twenty years. Don't imagine much has changed, though."

They came up to the boathouse, and Stanton tried the door.

"Locked, I imagine," Jack said. He held up the lantern to the small window of the boathouse, and Stanton and the Reverend peered in. Up on pallets they could see several barrels and various packages and boxes.

"This is a whole winter's supply of dry goods for the keeper," Jack said. He rattled the lock on the door. "Most of the fishermen around here are honest, but still, it wouldn't do well for the keeper to come down some mornin' and find the place cleaned out. Makes sense to lock it."

"Is there a path to get up there?" Reverend Morgan asked, peering up towards the tower of the lighthouse. It was slightly uphill from them and about 30 yards away.

"Aye, there's a path around to the left here if I can find it," Jack said, winding his way around the boathouse, with his lantern held out in front of him. Stanton and the Reverend followed behind. The rain was steady now, and the wind was becoming sporadically violent. The smell of the salt water was heavy in the moisture-laden air, and the men felt the cold and dampness more keenly as they got beyond the shelter of the boathouse and onto the open ground that lay before the tower.

"Blasted night for this," Stanton said, tilting his head down and pulling up the collar of his oilskin coat as he leaned into a particularly sharp gust of blowing rain.

"Can't really imagine that there'd be a *good* night for it," Jack replied.

Stanton mumbled something unintelligible, and the three continued on. Reverend Morgan looked up again at the lighthouse and watched as the main light traveled its endless circular route, making its small incision in the darkness that closed up again as fast as it had opened. He shielded his eyes with his hand and looked up again. Along with the main beam, there was also a small light on in the keeper's quarters.

"Watch your step, lads," Jack said, as they approached the foot of the tower. Jack held the lantern down so the three of them could see the granite steps that led up to the heavy oak doorway. They went up, and Stanton tried the iron handle on the door, but it didn't budge. He looked back at the other two.

"Well, there's the knocker," Jack said. "Are you going to use it?"

Stanton looked at Jack, who seemed to be just holding back a wry smile, and then he looked back at Reverend Morgan, who nodded solemnly. Stanton rapped the heavy iron knocker firmly three times, and then a fourth. He looked over to Jack and then to Reverend Morgan. Their faces were expressionless.

Reverend Morgan peered into the small, thick glass window just above the knocker, but all he could see was pitch black. "It'll take him a fair while to come down, I'd imagine," he said. The three of them waited for a full two minutes. Nothing.

"If he doesn't want to let us in, I don't suppose there's much we can do," Stanton said, with an air of resignation. Jack reached over and rapped the knocker against the iron plate, seven, eight times, in quick succession and with a great deal of force. The clanking of iron against iron reverberated out into the storm. Reverend Morgan looked over at Stanton, and Stanton shrugged his shoulders. They waited another minute.

"There," Reverend Morgan said, cocking his head and then putting his ear to the door. "I'm sure I heard something...yes…he's coming down…" A few moments later they all heard the sounds of someone stirring inside.

"There we go," Jack said, pointing up to a flickering light that now began to emanate from the small window.

"Is someone there?" a voice asked from inside the tower. "What do you want?" The three men immediately recognized the voice of their old friend.

"We'd really like to come in out of the rain, if you don't mind, Edmund," Jack said, in a friendly a manner, as if the two of them saw each other every day.

"Who is that?" Edmund asked. "What do you want?"

"It's Dan Morgan," the Reverend said. "I'm with Jack Hayes and William Stanton."

"What...what are you here for?"

"We just thought we'd stop by for a visit," Jack said. "It was really kind of a lark, a spur of the moment thing, you might say. You did say that we could visit you any time, as I recall."

"Yes...no...this isn't really a good time. I'm sorry. I do appreciate the visit, but I really can't see you. You should...you should just go back now, and come some other time. Next month, maybe, and let me know in advance," Edmund said. "I'll have a nice meal ready for you, if I have some time to plan."

"Edmund, my dear boy," Stanton said in the rich baritone that served him so well in the courtroom, "It's pouring rain out here, and the wind is whipping at us like the devil—you can't just turn us away."

"It's just not a good time," Edmund said, his voice rising in pitch. "Couldn't you have let me know you were coming?"

"Listen Edmund, just let us in to dry off a bit, and we'll be on our way as soon as the rain lets up. How does that sound?" Reverend Morgan said. 'Please, Edmund."

"Edmund," Stanton said loudly, "open the door, if you please." Jack looked away, back through the rain to the distant lights on the mainland, while Stanton and the Reverend exchanged solemn glances. There was a pause of several seconds, and then the iron lock clicked twice as it was turned, and the heavy oak door swung inward. The light of a lantern lit the stone and wood interior of the entrance-way, and also illuminated the familiar face of their old friend, Edmund.

"Of course I wouldn't turn you away," Edmund said. "It's just that I'm not...not really prepared for guests."

"What guests?" Stanton said, as he pulled back the hood of his coat and undid the front zipper. "We're your friends, you know." The three of them walked in out of the rain, and as they closed the door behind them the sound of the wind faded and was replaced by the heavy, ancient reverberations of the lighthouse's interior.

"I know you are," Edmund said. "It *is* good to see you, William." He patted Stanton firmly on the shoulder and chuckled. "Jack, you old sea dog, you look the same as ever." He took a step over and shook Jack's hand firmly. "I'm surprised you haven't visited me before, being out on the water as much as you are."

"I've been meaning to," Jack said, "but I've got my pots set on the other side of the bay, and it doesn't bring me over here too often. Not much time left at the end of a busy day, I find."

"Edmund," Reverend Morgan said heartily, "how have you been? Must've been over a year since we saw each other last."

"Daniel, yes...it has been a while..." Edmund said, smiling

politely and making brief eye contact with the Reverend, then turning away quickly. “Well now, let’s not stay down here. I’ve got a fire going up in the keeper’s berth, and I can at least get you a drink of some sort.” He shone his lantern towards the base of the spiral stone staircase. “I can’t say it’s a short climb, however.”

Edmund led the way up the stairs, with Jack following behind him and Stanton and the Reverend bringing up the rear. Jack and Edmund began talking about the weather and the sea over the last couple of weeks, and Stanton let them gain some distance from him and the Reverend.

“What do you think? Seems all right to me, although I couldn’t get a good look at him in that low light. But still, it’s our Edmund, as far as I can tell,” Stanton said quietly.

“Yes. Seems to be,” Reverend Morgan said, although he wasn’t sure. Of the three of them, he had been the closest to Edmund over the years, yet he seemed to have received the coolest welcome.

“It’s all nothing,” Stanton said, with an air of relief.

“You still with us, back there?” Edmund called from up above.

“Still coming,” the Reverend said loudly. “Right behind you.”

“Not much chance of a wrong turn for us, I should think,” Stanton joked as they continued up the spiral stairs.

***

“And welcome to my humble abode,” Edmund said. He held open the door from the stairwell to the keeper’s berth as his three guests walked through. There was a subdued fire burning in the fireplace, and between that and Edmund's lantern, the shadows danced on the wall as the men took off their rain gear. "Please, make yourselves comfortable," Edmund said, as he turned out two of the chairs from the small table that was just to the left of the fireplace and placed them next to his own rocking chair. "Please, Jack, take my chair. Let me take your coats, and you warm yourselves by the fire," he said, as he took their gear and hung it up on the wooden pegs just beside the doorway.

"This is quite cozy," Reverend Morgan said, rubbing his hands together in front of the fire, and looking around the room. "I can see how the solitude could be quite enjoyable. Could be a good chance to catch up on some hobbies, learn some new things. You still play the violin, Edmund?"

"No, haven't kept up with that, I'm afraid," Edmund said. "Anything to drink? All I have is bourbon."

"That'll do," Stanton said, "to warm a body on a night like this one."

"Yes," Edmund said quickly, "it is a bit of a rough night for a visit. Not that I'm unhappy to see you, but what made you come out in this miserable weather?" Jack stood up as Edmund came over to him holding a tray with four glasses on it and a bottle of whiskey.

"Well, we had planned this for a while," Jack said, "and I couldn't very well let these landlubbers tell me it was too rainy a night to go out on the water now, could I?"

"No, I don't suppose you could," Edmund said, smiling, as he poured Jack a shot of whiskey and then did the same for Stanton and the Reverend.

"Now that hits the spot," the Reverend said, taking a small sip. "So tell us Edmund, how have things been up here? Must get quite lonely at times...."

"Indeed," Stanton said, keeping his tone jovial. "And as I recall, Edmund, you were never the solitary, introspective type."

"No, I never was," Edmund said, "and maybe that was part of my problem. I was always looking for the next event, the next party, the next new show. Never took the time to think things through, to get to know myself. Taking this job has been quite good for me, actually. I don't think I realized how much I needed something like this. I have a lot of time here. I've been reading a lot, doing a bit of painting."

He gestured over to an easel in the corner, and Reverend Morgan could just make out a half-finished oil portrait of an old woman with a cruel smile.

"It's a bit like an extended vacation here, really," Edmund continued. "It's good to calm the nerves, I'd say."

"Ah, I don't think I'd last two days up here by myself," Stanton said. "I'd go crazy as a loon."

"Yes, I imagine you would, William," Edmund said, grinning, and for just a moment Reverend Morgan thought that he could see the old Edmund, the one he had shared so much of his youth with. But that sensation faded as quickly as it had come for the Reverend.

"But really, it's quite pleasant up here. I have no complaints," Edmund said.

"But still, it must be a bit unnerving," the Reverend said.

Edmund turned to Reverend Morgan, smiling slightly. "How

do you mean, Daniel?"

"Well, with the bodies that have been found. Rather strange. Certainly seems like something is amiss."

Jack watched carefully for Edmund's response.

"Oh yes, I did hear something about that," Edmund said. "Two women, did I hear? Drowned?"

"There was six bodies found, altogether," Jack said, not looking up as he sipped his whiskey.

"Six?" Edmund said.

"Aye, six," Jack continued. "And they didn't drown."

"Didn't drown?" Edmund said. He took another sip of his whiskey as he walked over to the fireplace. He picked up the poker and broke up what remained of one of the smaller logs into coals. "I hadn't heard that." He continued poking around in the fire. "What did they die of?"

"No one's said for sure," Jack said. "Very odd, though. Very odd. I'm surprised you didn't hear more about it. Most of the bodies were found right around this island."

"Yes," Edmund said. "Well, I often go weeks at a time up here without talking to anyone." He stood up and put the poker back into its place on the rack. "Only when the supply boat comes over with provisions, and even then they often just leave things in the boathouse without bothering me. I'm afraid I'm about the last person to keep up on current news."

"Real curious, it was," Jack said. "I saw one of the bodies myself. Looked like it was drained of blood."

"Yes, they tell me that the sea can do strange things to bodies in a very short time," Edmund said.

"I've been at sea my whole life, as you all know," Jack continued. "I've been involved in more than one search for a lost fisherman, or a man gone overboard in the night. Found a few bodies, but none that looked like this poor girl."

Edmund poured himself another shot of whiskey and took a long, slow sip. He paused for a moment and then turned to face his guests. "Well, I guess you learn something new every day. I wasn't aware that being a fisherman qualified you as a coroner."

"Jack's just stating his experience, Edmund," Stanton pressed. "No need to get irritable about it."

"Ah, yes, pressing the advantage, eh William? Just like in court? Really, if you're trying to accuse me of something, why don't you just come out and say it?"

Stanton smiled humorlessly and reached into the inside jacket of his coat, pulling out his pipe and tobacco. "What would we be accusing you of?" he asked, as he packed his pipe.

"I really don't know," Edmund said. "Just because tourists with no experience on the water come up here boating and have an accident, I don't see how that relates to me."

"Edmund, you're our friend," Reverend Morgan continued. "We're worried about you. That's all. Do you need help with anything?"

"Help?" Edmund said, walking over to the window and looking out over the sea. "I'm afraid *you* really don't have any help to offer, Daniel. Fairy tales and silly myths?" He turned to the Reverend. "I know you, Daniel. You're not stupid. How do you still hold on to those ridiculous scriptures of yours? Do you honestly believe that mumbo-jumbo? Do you think there's any real power in that?

"There is a great power in that," the Reverend said calmly. "Just as there is great power in the living God."

Edmund laughed and turned around, his eyes shining. "I've *seen* power, Daniel. Real power. Power that works in *this* world, not in some distant fairlyland."

"I'm sorry, Edmund," Reverend Morgan said with an air of resignation. "What did your new friends promise you? What were you offered in exchange for your soul?"

"For my soul?" Edmund said, grinning. "Now that's a bit melodramatic. There *is* no such thing as a soul, Daniel. I realize that you can never accept that, but that's reality. We are material creatures, in a material universe. Modern science confirms that more fully each year."

"We are material creatures," Reverend Morgan said. "But that's not all we are. What *did* they promise you, Edmund?"

"They didn't promise anything, Daniel—they delivered it," Edmund said. He looked out at the faces of his old friends: the stoic, weathered countenance of Jack, the melancholy resolution of Daniel, and the nervous indignation of Stanton. "Ah, so serious, all of you. You really have no idea what you're on about, do you? Fair enough, then. Some kind of demonstration is warranted."

He put his glass down on the table, and backed up against the stone wall of the tower, smiling fiercely. He leaned back against the wall, with his arms at his side and his palms turned backwards. He touched his palms to the wall. "Oh yes, this really works better with these off," he said, slipping off his shoes and socks. He brought one knee up and put the sole of one foot back against the wall, and started crawling straight up.

"Good God!" Stanton cried.

Edmund moved up the wall steadily, alternating his hands and feet, all the while keeping eye contact with his guests. His motion was unnatural, but perhaps even more disturbingly, not entirely inhuman.

"Itsy bitsy spider, climbed up the water spout," Edmund sang, grinning perversely. "I never read about Peter or Paul being able to do this, did you, Daniel? Were Augustine or Aquinas granted the strength of five men? Could St. Francis hear conversations from a half mile away?"

"No, he couldn't," Reverend Morgan said.

Edmund stopped about fifteen feet up the wall and looked down at the three. "It's really too bad. Too bad that I have to dispose of you all. I would have liked to offer you the opportunity to join me—especially you, Daniel—but I'd need permission, and I don't think I'm going to have the opportunity to obtain that."

"You'd just kill us then, like those women?"

"Look, they were just prostitutes," Edmund said. "Not really your churchgoing type, Reverend. But no, I won't kill you like them. I see I don't need to draw further attention to myself here. Unfortunately, you three were out on the water tonight, and your craft was hit by a much larger boat. You all died from some combination of blunt trauma and drowning. Quite tragic, really."

"I'm not sure that's how it's going to happen," Jack said, calmly drawing his Colt revolver from inside his coat.

"Ah Jack, always the man of action," Edmund said, looking down. "I'm afraid that's not going to be of much use to you, however."

"No?" Jack asked, as he calmly opened the cylinder, checked it, and spun it around, locking it back into place. He held it up with a steady hand, aimed at Edmund. "Not even with wooden bullets?"

***

Several hours later, they were back in town at the pub. Jack Hayes picked up his whiskey glass and took a sip, while William Stanton downed his in one gulp.

"He was our friend, you know," Stanton said.

"I think our friend died long before tonight," Reverend Morgan said. "The creature we destroyed was someone else entirely."

"I don't know, Reverend," Jack said. "There was still some of him in there, I'd wager. That part just wasn't calling the shots anymore, I'd say."

The "Red Rooster" sign outside the pub banged in the wind, and the barmaid came over to their table.

"Get you another drink, boys?" she asked. "Oh, looks like it's coming down harder out there," she said, peering out the window into the street. "Say, if you stay for another round, Fiona O'Donnell is going to start singing with the band. She's really quite good."

"Sure," Reverend Morgan said. "Another round for my friends."

"Will do," The barmaid said cheerily, and walked back towards the bar. There was hardly an empty seat in the pub now, and boisterous conversations and laughter were taking place in every corner except the one.

"What will they say when the authorities go and check on the lighthouse?" Stanton asked.

"What can they say?" Jack said. "There's nothing to find. You saw what happened to his body. They'll just find an empty lighthouse."

"I'm sure there will be all kinds of speculation," Reverend Morgan said thoughtfully. "Another local mystery."

"It'll die down, soon enough," Jack said quietly, taking another sip of his whiskey. "In ten years barely anyone will remember it. That's just the way things go."

To Float is to Dream

Colonel Tak Yoshita half-dreamed that he was twelve years old again, floating in the gentle waters of Lake Shojiko. By mid-September the faint chill of autumn would be in the air, but the water would still be warm for another few weeks. He and his pals Hiro and Etsuko would challenge each other to see who could tread water the longest. Hiro was the strongest swimmer, but Etsuko was such a tomboy, and she never backed down. After a while, they had each gotten so good at it that it wasn't really a competition; they would just hover easily in the warm lake water, and talk about things, and laugh, and dream about the future. The grand countenance of Mount Fuji would look down on them in benevolent silence, and they would float for what seemed like hours. At the base of the mountain, some of the leaves would just be starting to change color.

***

The cold wave broke and smashed against his face, and Tak was awake. Floating. His life jacket was inflated, and it had kept his head above water. He remembered the giant shape in the sea and something about ejecting, but not much else. He felt himself rhythmically rising and falling with the movement of the ocean, and along with the salt water that had crusted on his lips he was aware of the copper-sweet taste of blood. He ran his hand over his face and head. No major cuts that he could find, and other than a dull headache, no pain. He wiped his nose on his wrist, and saw a streak of blood. *A bloody nose.* Not much to complain about, all things considered. He looked out over the vast expanse of water and considered his situation. Maybe sharks, he thought. He cracked a half smile. *Sharks*. That was really kind of funny.

He had no idea how long he had been in the water, but it didn't really matter much. He knew he could float as long as he needed to. He cocked his head as he thought he heard something. *A small engine*?

"Hey, he's alive!" A man's voice came from a distance over the water behind Tak, speaking English. "I told you guys he wasn't that low when he bailed!"

"Nice. Easier to replace the jets than the pilots," another man said.

"Get him in quick," the first said. The man cupped his hands to his mouth and yelled to Tak. "Just a minute, buddy. We're gonna get you out of there!"

Tak tried to turn around in the water to see who was speaking, but when he kicked hard he felt a searing pain in his right leg. He was still able to maneuver a bit, but he had a good idea that the leg was broken. As he slowly rotated in the water, he saw the small black inflatable boat approaching. It cut its engine and drifted up next to him. From the uniforms, Tak recognized the three men on board as sailors of the U.S. Navy.

"Hey, you speak English, buddy? You all right?" The man was thin and wiry, with orange-red hair.

"Some English," Tak said. "Okay. Right leg...broken," he said, pointing down into the water with his right hand.

"He's got a broken leg," the seaman said, as he and his companion lifted Tak out of the water and into the boat. "Yeah, that one. Watch out for it. Easy...there we go. Hey buddy, you cut your chute off when you hit the water?"

"Don't...remember," Tak said.

"Well, I guess you must have. Good thing—that'll drag you right under."

A low, bellowing roar reverberated across the water, so bass-heavy that all the men could feel it in their chests. Tak looked out from the boat and could just make out the dark shape of the giant beast Jizorah breaking the surface, at least five kilometers out to sea.

"Coming in...or going out?" Tak said.

"Huh?" the red-haired seaman said.

"Jizorah," Tak said. "I...lose direction..."

"Oh, yeah—going out! Back out to sea. He didn't make landfall at all. We held him off this time, and drove him back. Word just came in, no civilian casualties in Yokohama. Nice job, buddy—we had a good day!"

***

Back on the deck of the USS Providence, Tak lay on his stretcher and lit a cigarette as a Navy medic gently adjusted the splint on his leg.

“This won’t be too bad,” the medic said. He was a tall, heavy-set man with kindly eyes. “It was a clean break—should heal normally.” The medic patted him on the shoulder, and then moved to the next wounded man on a stretcher to the left.

Tak leaned up on his elbow, and looked out over the deck and across the sea. In the fading light, far in the distance he saw the flickering blue beam of a maser cannon from one of the battleships. A second later he heard its high-pitched whine and another roar from Jizorah, and he wondered whatever became of his friends Hiro and Etsuko.

Even Closer Than the Sea

"I'm telling you, I'm gonna see me a Kraut sub one of these days," Private Jim Barrett said as he peered through his spotting scope out over the cold, gray Atlantic. "Do we get some kind of bonus if we see one, Cap?"

"This goddamn *station* is your bonus, Private," Captain Lodge said. "You're fighting the war in a tower. Stateside. Think maybe that's a little easier than Sicily, or Tarawa? Nobody's shooting at you here." His clear, baritone voice added some power to his slight frame. At twenty-seven, Captain Wendell Lodge was a few years older than the three men under his command, and he used that age difference to buttress his authority when he needed to.

"Hey, I'm not complaining, Cap—I'm just asking." Barrett said, grinning. "Although it's probably a lot warmer in those places than it is here. Damn, I thought it was supposed to be mild down here in the winter. This is as cold as anything I felt growing up."

"Ah, you Vermonters—always complaining about the weather," Private Rich Ingram said. "This is just Massachusetts cold—it ain't *real* cold. Try New York. You do some logging around Saranac or Lake Placid this time of year, and you'll know what cold is." He hunched over slightly to look through his own scope to the east, out over Massachusetts Bay.

"Man, how did we get stuck in here with these hillbillies, Cap?" Private Dan McCauley asked. "Right from the goddamn woods, or cow barn, or whatever the hell they do out there. I don't care where you're from, this is cold," the private said.

It *was* cold, Capt. Lodge thought. He took a draw from his cigarette, and pulled the collar up on his heavy wool coat and buttoned the top button. This posting sure seemed a lot nicer a few months ago, in September, when the leaves on the trees were bright gold and red and the gentle breeze that blew in off the ocean was pleasant, instead of biting and severe.

The mission here was simple enough: a steel and concrete watch tower had been put up right behind the old granite quarry in Stonewater, Massachusetts. The town was essentially a small peninsula, jutting out from the coast into the ocean some thirty-plus miles north of Boston. The tower was only a hundred yards or so from the sea and provided an ideal lookout over the bay and down the coast. German planes and surface ships were a possibility, although not that likely at this point in the war. After the Battle of Britain, the Luftwaffe was in no position to mount any serious threat against the continental United States.

The real threat came from the U-boats. Things had gotten better since the "Black May" of '43, when the Allies lost all those ships in the Atlantic, but the German submarines were still a potent adversary. And along with the attacks on the shipping convoys that supplied the lifeline to Britain, there was also the possibility of the U-boats landing spies and saboteurs on the coast. This tower in Stonewater didn't have any artillery—their job was to sight and confirm targets, and call in the information to the shore batteries in Nahant and Boston. Easy enough.

"You think there's anything out there, Cap? We've been here a couple months, and all we've seen are a few whales, some friendlies, and a bunch of fishing boats," McCauley said.

"They're out there," Lodge said. He slowly cranked the handle on his tripod-mounted M1910 azimuth telescope, panning a few degrees towards the northeast. "Maybe not many, but you can bet they're coming up for a look-see here and there. Hell, our subs are doing the same thing on the coast of France."

"Yeah, but ain't we planning some big invasion there?" Private Ingram said, taking his cigar out of his mouth. "I thought they were pulling back at this point."

That was mostly true, Lodge thought. The Nazi's "Operation Sea Lion" plan for invading England was just about forgotten, and if they weren't able to take England, they sure as hell weren't going to land in force on the East Coast of the United States.

"Just keep your eyes open and pay attention," Capt. Lodge said. "The war's not over yet. Not by a long shot." Lodge stood up straight and looked out to sea with his naked eyes. He took his left glove off and cupped his hand to his mouth, blowing warm air on it. *Damn, his fingers were cold.* Some warmth did make it up to the top of the tower from the heated quarters on the ground floor, but not much. At any rate, with the wide horizontal viewing slits that needed to be kept open, they weren't going to be walking around in short-sleeves up in the tower any time soon. And it didn't really matter how likely an invasion was or was not, Lodge thought—his orders were to man this tower and observe the coastal waters, and that's what they were going to do.

"And don't forget what happened there off Long Island," Lodge said. "Nazis brought a U-boat close to shore and dropped off those spies."

"Yeah," Pvt. Barrett said, "any of them land here and they're going to have a pretty short stay."

"Oh, watch out—we got Sergeant York up here," Ingram said, laughing.

"Hey, I'm not saying we shoot it out or anything," Barrett said, "but if they resist, well...."

"Let's worry more about spotting the U-boat first, and letting the battery guns in Nahant do their job," Lodge said.

"Wouldn't that be great?" Ingram said. "Seeing a whole salvo land out there and take one out."

Capt. Lodge looked at his watch. It was almost noon. "Barrett, take your lunch break," he said. "Be back in forty-five."

"Hey, go down and check the ice on the quarry," Ingram said. "If it gets thick enough we could play a little hockey down there at night. It's been this cold for two weeks, it should be frozen solid."

"Yeah," McCauley said, "why don't you run right out to the middle and jump up and down to make sure?"

"You guys better *hope* we don't play hockey," Barrett said. "Half my family's French Canadian, you know—we invented it."

"Don't get too cocky," Ingram said. "I'm sure Cap can take us all. He played at Harvard. Didn't you, Cap?"

"I did," Lodge said. "That was a few years ago, though."

"Oh, college boy, huh?" Barrett said. "Well, I got a cousin that plays for Montreal. The Habs, that is. Pros. I bet we could play some real shinny down there, and I'd take it easy on you."

"We got the sticks, but none of us here have skates," Lodge said.

"I'm sure we can round some up in town," Ingram said.

"You sure you want to go back after last Saturday?" McCauley said. "Massachusetts girls don't like you out-of-staters, you know."

"The girls liked us fine," Barrett said. "It was their boyfriends who were the problem."

"Go take your lunch. I want to keep us on schedule," Lodge said. He took another long draw on his cigarette, and then dropped it on the cement floor and put it out with the toe of his boot. He actually liked each of the men under his command, and it was hard to refrain from joining in with their jokes and antics. But he knew his job wasn't to be their pal. This was war, and even if they weren't in the middle of combat, discipline and a command structure had to be maintained.

"I'm going to grab a bite and some coffee first, but I'll check out the ice," Barrett said. He made his way over to the ladder stairs and eased himself down.

No granite had been excavated from the quarry for about twenty years, but the effects of the old industry were all around. The main quarry was a rough oval about a hundred-fifty yards long by twenty yards wide, and went down to a depth of about ten yards. A natural spring had gradually filled nearly the whole pit with fresh water, and the easternmost lip of the quarry was only about twenty yards from the rocky shore and the great Atlantic. It had been cold enough over the last couple weeks that some faint ice had even formed on the shoreline, despite the saltwater and steady waves. The freshwater in the quarry, however, had frozen nicely over the whole surface.

Pvt. Barrett came down the final flight of stairs, and into the main living quarters. As he opened the door, he was met with a welcome rush of warm air. He immediately took his gloves off, went over to the wood stove and rubbed his hands together over the soothing heat radiating from the cast iron stove. The warmth soon penetrated down to his bones, and a quick shiver of pleasure went down his spine. He put the coffee pot on the stove, and went over to the cupboard and made himself a ham and cheese sandwich.

"Almost out of wood—I guess I'm the only one that notices that," he said to nobody in particular. He stepped out the back doorway and to the small woodshed a couple yards away. There were about three cords neatly stacked in the shed, and he grabbed an armful of split wood and brought it back inside, putting the pieces in the wood bin. He took another big gulp of the hot coffee and finished the ham sandwich. He put his gloves and wool cap back on, and looked at the big army thermometer next to the door. Still just 18 degrees out there.

He walked down the path from the watchtower to the quarry, about thirty yards down the small hill that the tower was situated on. He briefly looked up at the tower, but apparently nobody up there was paying attention to him, or he would have heard some choice comments and less-than-helpful advice by now. He reached the edge of the quarry. It had been a strange late autumn/early winter that year—extremely cold temperatures off and on since early November, but hardly a flake of snow had fallen. The water level in the quarry was about four or five feet below the granite lip, and the ice had formed a clear cover. Barrett got down on all fours and peered down. The ground was bare and frozen solid, the grass whitish-green and crisp—and the cold combined with the lack of snow had had the curious effect of making the ice on the quarry surface crystal clear. The water was probably twenty-five feet deep below the ice, and the walls of the quarry were almost vertical. He wasn't too keen on putting his whole weight on the ice, then breaking through and sinking straight to the bottom in his heavy, woolen winter clothes.

He leaned further over the edge and looked down. He could just make out the bottom edge of the ice, and it looked to be a solid six inches. He had enough experience on the ponds and brooks near his family farm outside of Burlington, Vermont to know that this was probably more than solid enough to walk on. Still, it didn't hurt to be careful. He shifted around as if he was going back down a ladder from a roof, and slowly lowered himself down onto the ice, supporting most of his weight with his hands on the granite edge.

"Don't be such a little girl—just walk out to the middle!" Barrett looked up at the tower to see who was yelling, but he couldn't make out who was at the window. His view was partially obscured by the leafless branches of a couple of tall trees on the edge of the quarry. It sounded like McCauley.

"Get your ass down here if you want to try it!" Barrett yelled back. There was a response from the tower, but he couldn't clearly make it out. His feet were on the ice, and it was supporting about half of his weight. Seemed sturdy enough. He carefully let the rest of his weight down, keeping his hands ready to grab the rock edge if the ice did give way. He gently rose up and down a couple times, and he didn't hear any cracks or pings. He walked out about five feet, and again bounced gently. Everything seemed fine.

"What's the word?" McCauley yelled from up in the tower.

"Seems pretty good," Barrett said to himself. He turned and gave the guys in the tower a thumbs up.

He took several short, quick steps on the ice and then slid for a few feet; he began to make his way across the quarry like this. This was going to be great for hockey, he thought, even if they didn't have skates. The ice was perfect: smooth as glass and thick as you could ask for. Maybe they could set up a couple bonfires here and there at night, get some two-by-fours out of the shed and build a couple of goals. Barrett continued alternately walking and sliding across the ice, heading towards the far end of the quarry closest to the ocean.

The sky was a dull gray, and the air coming in off the sea was heavy with moisture. It felt like there would be some snow falling by early this evening, Barrett thought. He had gone about two thirds of the length of the quarry when he felt the first crack. That strange, slightly metallic "ping" that goes through cracking ice reverberated in the winter air. He had been on pond and lake ice before when he had heard this sound, and he didn't panic. Usually it was just the ice subtly adjusting to the added weight, and there was no serious danger of it giving way.

He did stop, however. As he scanned across the whole surface, he noticed something he hadn't seen before. There was a hole in the ice, about ten feet in diameter, fifteen or twenty feet from the far edge of the quarry. It wasn't jagged; it looked like the ice around the edge of the hole was quite thin, as if it had been melted through. Probably one of the natural springs that fed the quarry was just below the spot, Barrett reasoned, and the water there was moving just enough to keep from freezing. Oh well, this wasn't a big problem—they still had the whole rest of the quarry, which was bigger than the ice the Bruins played on at Boston Garden. They could just put a length of rope or something down so that they'd know not to go any further in that direction.

Pvt. Barrett resumed his shuffle across the ice. He looked down again and he really couldn't recall ever having seen ice on any body of water that was so clear. It was a little too deep to distinctly make out anything on the bottom, though—all he could see was just the dull gray of the water underneath. He walked on a little further when something caught his attention. It was something under his feet, under the ice. *Movement?* He wasn't sure, just something he barely noticed out of the corner of his eye. *There were probably fish in here under the ice.* He looked down carefully, but nothing was stirring. But there was something there. It was just a foot or so under the ice, but he could make it out. It was black and slender—probably only a couple inches wide, but it was long; it seemed to stretch ahead for several feet. He leaned down to get a closer look. Whatever it was, it wasn't moving. *Just a branch or weed caught here when the water froze, maybe?*

He walked forward, following along the increasing length of the black shape. Ten, twelve...fifteen feet. It was sort of cylindrical, and getting wider—now probably a foot and a half in diameter. Barrett couldn't make out any details at all, just an elongated black form under the ice. He took a few steps more, and had some difficulty processing exactly what he was seeing. The cylinder was apparently attached to something larger, and as he kept walking he found himself standing over a huge black oval, probably ten feet wide and twelve feet long. *What the hell is that? Some tarp or piece of rubber that got blown into the water and sunk a bit, and then froze solid?* He walked around the outline of the object to get a better sense of its size, and then he got down on his hands and knees and brought his face close to the clear ice to see if he could make out any details. Nope, just a black...something...under the ice. With the knuckles of his right hand, he knocked on the ice several times. The entire bulk of the black object jerked underneath him.

"Holy shit!" Barrett hoarsely yelled. "Shit!" He stood up quickly, almost jumping, his heart thumping heavily in his chest.

He began to step back, and he saw the body of the thing move again under the ice, and its tail—that's what he now understood it had to be—flexed in a sideways, serpentine manner. Pvt. Barrett's mind reeled. He didn't come from a fishing town like McCauley—he was from inland, the mountains. But he instinctively felt with a fair degree of certainty that this wasn't something that was regularly encountered, even here. *What the hell, a giant tadpole*? On some level Barrett knew that didn't make any sense, but that was all he could come up with. Think. *Think.* It's fresh water—what gets that big in fresh water? A sturgeon, something else? This was more than twenty feet from head to tail if it was an inch—it wasn't a goddamn sturgeon. The ocean wasn't that many yards away—maybe there was some underground connection, or the sea water got close enough at high tide that it was able to get into the quarry? *That WHAT was able to get into the quarry?* It wasn't a shark, it wasn't a seal. It wasn't anything he knew. He scrambled back to the edge of the ice as best he could without slipping, and felt some comfort when his hands reached the solid granite wall. He looked back and down at the ice, but the angle was too severe to be able to make out anything clearly.

He pulled himself up onto the granite, and then walked a few feet up onto the grass. He looked up at the tower for a moment, and then took a step back towards the ice and scanned it again, trying to get a glimpse of the thing.

The air was cold and damp, and it had begun to spit a fine snow. He looked quickly out to sea, then back to the ice and up to the tower again, rubbing his hands together. All he could hear was the cold, brittle wind easing in, and the faint, rhythmic breaking of the waves onto the big sea rocks at the shore. As he looked back towards the ice he realized that he was alone in this. No one else had seen it, and no one else knew that he had seen it. Barrett was momentarily ashamed at his own fear, and the fact that his heart was still pounding. He took a deep breath and exhaled. Still, he didn't have to have all the answers, did he? Maybe this whole thing was something stupid, something that he couldn't see at the moment. If he called the others down, maybe they could explain it. Sure, they'd get on his case and tease him about it, but that wasn't so bad. That wasn't so bad at all.

"Hey, Cap!" Barrett called up to the tower. "Cap!" There was no answer. "Hey Cap!"

"Yeah? What's going on?" Capt. Lodge yelled from the window in the tower. His voice seemed slightly distant and muffled in the heavy air.

"Cap, maybe you should come down here..." Barrett said, cupping his hands as he yelled up to the tower. He tried desperately to keep his voice steady and unemotional.

"What is it?"

"There's something here...under the ice. I don't know what it is. It's big. I think...I think it's moving," Barrett said.

"What'd he say, Cap?" Ingram asked. "He see some animal or something?"

"Under the ice—I think that's what he said. Something moving," Lodge said. "McCauley, go down and see what he's yapping about."

"Sure thing, Cap," McCauley said. He grabbed his wool gloves from the shelf, put them on, and went down the ladder. He was soon at the bottom and heading out the door of the tower. He saw Barrett standing on the edge of the quarry, looking down, and walked over to him.

“Hey, what gives? You see a deer or something?”

“No” Barrett said. His eyes were firmly fixed on the ice as he slowly paced along the edge, scanning for another sign of the thing. He barely noticed McCauley next to him. McCauley followed a few steps behind, looking at the ice himself and trying to see what might be of interest down there.

“Didn’t you go out on the ice? What was it, too thin?” McCauley asked, as they both kept treading slowly around the edge of the frozen quarry.

“No....it was plenty thick,” Barrett said. “There’s something under there. Under the ice.”

“Like what?” McCauley asked. “You must have just seen a fish or something. Snapping turtle, maybe. They can move around under the ice.”

“It wasn’t a goddamn turtle,” Barrett said. “It’s *big*.” His eyes were drawn to movement to his right. “There!” His shoulder jerked as he flung his arm out, pointing.

McCauley was silent as he turned to where Barrett was pointing, his eyes trying to fix on just what was there. And then he saw it, about twenty feet out. The shape was indistinct, but there was definitely a dark form moving underneath the ice, and it wasn’t small.

“Holy cow, what the hell is that?” he said, as he took a couple quick steps towards the edge, and then got down on all fours as he looked out. The form came a bit closer to shore, and then turned sharply and slowly headed back out towards the middle, until McCauley couldn’t make it out any more.

"You tell me," Barrett said. "You're the fisherman, right?" Barrett had heard more than enough of McCauley's stories of growing up in his New Bedford whaling town, where everyone knew everything about the ocean—a lot more than he, an ignorant landlubber, would ever know. Barrett took some pleasure in the fact that McCauley was unsure of himself. He appreciated the company.

"You got me," McCauley said, still scanning the ice. "If we were out on the open water I'd say a shark or big skate, maybe, but freshwater...and under the ice? Doesn't make any goddamn sense. Maybe it came in from the ocean?" He looked over to the far side of the quarry, trying to get a sense of the logistics. He didn't sound very confident of his theory.

"I don't know where it came from, but it's not a shark. I was standing right over it. Too long, and the wrong shape. It's got a big round body, and a long thin tail, "Barrett said.

"How long, overall?"

"I'd say twenty, twenty-five feet," Barrett said.

McCauley looked up at the tower. "I'm going to go get my M-1," he said, as he turned and half jogged back towards the door.

"Hey, bring me my .45!" Barrett yelled after him, and McCauley grunted in the affirmative.

McCauley flew up the four flights of stairs to the top floor of the tower, and quickly came through the door. "Cap, you gotta come down and see this!"

"What is it?" Ingram asked. "Barrett fall through?"

"No, but he's right—there *is* something down there. It's under the ice."

Capt. Lodge was bent over the big azimuth telescope, looking out over the assigned coordinates. "What's under the ice?" Lodge said, with a tone not unlike that of an adult talking to an over-excited child. He didn't look up from his scope.

"Cap, there's something weird down there—I don't know what it is." McCauley realized he was sounding overly dramatic, and he composed himself. "I'm requesting permission to investigate, sir."

Capt. Lodge sighed, and looked up. McCauley wasn't smiling as he usually did when he was horsing around—which was often—and he seemed genuinely upset.

"I think you should come down and take a look too, sir. Something's not right," McCauley said.

"I can go down, Cap," Ingram said. He had no idea what was going on, but he figured it had to be more exciting than staring out endlessly at the same gray waves, and writing the exact same entry in the logbook. He looked through the slot down to where Barrett was standing at the edge of the quarry.

"Stay at your post, Private, and pay attention to your job," Lodge said. He stood up straight, and buttoned up his coat. "I'll go down and check it out." He put on his wool cap, and pulled the lined ear flaps down. McCauley was impatient, and Capt. Lodge deliberately made him wait. Lodge took his pen and wrote a few lines in his logbook, and then carefully put his gloves on. Pvt. McCauley looked at him with annoyance, and Lodge raised his eyebrows and, after adjusting his gloves, extended his upturned palm towards the door. McCauley sighed and shook his head, and headed out the door and down the stairs, with Capt. Lodge right behind him.

As they came down the stairs into the main living quarters, McCauley went to the armory, which was really just a closet in the back where the weapons and ammunition were stored. Lodge was going to question the need for weapons, but kept silent. While McCauley could be quite obnoxious and annoying, Lodge had never known him to overreact, nor be prone to exaggeration. Capt. Lodge followed McCauley over to the weapon rack in the closet. McCauley pulled his M1 carbine off the rack, shoved one clip into the rifle and put another in his pocket. Lodge took his own Colt M1911 pistol from the rack, and slid the magazine into the grip of the weapon with a resounding click. He put the pistol into the holster on its belt, and clasped the belt around his waist. McCauley also grabbed Barret's Colt, inserted a magazine and put the pistol in its belt and holster.

The snowflakes floating out of the gray sky were bigger now, and the wind was not letting up as Lodge and McCauley approached the quarry and Barrett.

"Did you see it again?" McCauley asked. He handed Barrett the sidearm, and Barrett clipped the belt and holster around his waist.

"Yeah, it came close to shore again a minute ago," Barrett said. "I don't know where it is now."

"So what exactly are we dealing with?" Capt. Lodge asked. He was by nature a practical man, and he needed information before he could assess this situation.

"I don't know, Cap, but this is really weird. I've never seen anything like this. Maybe we should call in for somebody," Barrett said.

"Yeah," McCauley said. "I've spent a lot of time around the water, Cap. I've never seen anything like this before."

"I'm not quite getting why this is a concern for us. We've got our orders, and we're not running a marine biology lab," Capt. Lodge said. McCauley and Barrett were looking intently at the ice, and despite his own words, Lodge found himself with some degree of curiosity. Ingram was manning the tower—he was okay up there by himself. Maybe this was a good test of his command, of his ability to appraise an unknown situation and deal with it. He knew that the men under him were less than impressed with his Harvard credentials, and while they liked him and respected the rank, he wanted more than that. He scanned the ice.

"There it is," he said. His voice was calm and steady, and belied the internal reaction he was experiencing. The dark shape slowly approached them, and then turned, its undulating tail propelling the grotesquely shaped thing smoothly through the frigid water under the ice. Lodge saw that they weren't exaggerating. The thing was huge, whatever it was. They weren't wrong about that.

"Barrett, you said the ice is strong?" Lodge asked.

"Yeah, the ice is strong here, Cap," Barrett said. "You're not... going out on it?"

"We all are. Any reason we shouldn't?" Capt. Lodge asked.

Barrett hesitated. He couldn't really think of any reason that wouldn't sound cowardly if he said it out loud. He shook his head. Captain Lodge started walking around the rim of the quarry over to the left, towards the far end that was furthest away from the sea.

"You're fine down there, Cap, but the ice gets thin and opens up at the other end," Barrett said.

"I noticed that," Lodge replied. He reached the far end of the quarry, and he waved for Barrett to come down to where he was.

Barrett understood. Just like herding sheep back home—Lodge wanted to flush the thing out to the other end, into the open water. He had no idea what they were going to do after that, but it felt good to have some kind of plan.

Captain Lodge looked around, and saw what he needed: on the edge of the quarry were the hockey sticks that Barrett had gotten from town last week. He grabbed them, and then he lowered himself over the lip of the granite and onto the ice.

"Come here," Lodge said, motioning Barrett and McCauley down to him.

"What, Cap?" McCauley asked.

"Come on, get down here," Capt. Lodge said. The two were hesitant, but McCauley slung his M1 over his shoulder, and lowered himself down onto the ice. Barrett followed. Lodge handed them each a hockey stick. "We'll try to drive it out to that open water at the other end—at least we'll see what it is. Spread out so we can cover the width."

The three took their places on the ice, with Capt. Lodge in the middle and McCauley and Barrett on the sides. At Capt. Lodge's signal, they began to move ahead slowly, tapping their sticks on the ice. The tapping seemed muffled and reverberated strangely in the cold, heavy air, and the breaking of the waves on the nearby sea rocks was the only other sound. The snow continued to fall steadily.

"There it is," Capt. Lodge said softly. McCauley and Barrett stopped and looked at Lodge. The massive bulk of the thing was slowly moving directly towards him. He tapped the stick firmly on the ice, and just before it was directly under him, the thing turned sharply, reversing its direction.

"He doesn't like that," Lodge said, and he felt a subtle thrill. "If you see him coming, start tapping. Let's keep going."

They slowly but steadily made their way forward. Each time the thing would try to circle back, one of the men would tap their stick on the ice, blocking its way. Lodge speculated that maybe the thing was hypersensitive to the noise or vibrations, but for whatever reason, the tapping always made it turn around. They were about half way down the length of the ice, and Capt. Lodge could see the spot of open water up ahead.

"Make some noise," he said, as he began smacking the ice steadily with his stick. "We'll drive it right up there." McCauley and Barrett did as he asked and the three of them advanced. The thing seemed to be moving more quickly now. The sluggishness that they noticed when they first saw it was gone now, replaced by an increasing agitation and willfulness of movement.

They kept tapping, as they were now about ten yards from the open ice ahead. McCauley continued on the far side of the quarry, tapping with the stick in his right hand, but as he did so he climbed up from the ice onto the stone wall of the quarry. He unslung his M1 and held that in his left hand, as he leaned over and kept hitting the ice with his stick in the other hand, and continued forward.

"If it comes to the open water, I can get a shot at it, Cap," he half whispered. Barrett stayed in his position, and kept pace with Capt. Lodge. They could see the thing ahead of them, circling, weaving to and fro.

"Let's pour it on," Capt. Lodge said, and he began hitting the ice hard and fast with his hockey stick, again and again. Barrett and McCauley followed suit.

Capt. Lodge was never quite sure exactly what happened next.

The thing darted in front of him, and moved at an incredible speed towards the open water.

"Get ready, McCauley—it's coming up!" Lodge yelled. McCauley dropped the hockey stick and swung his carbine around. The thing came out of the water with a speed and power that the men would not have thought possible. It looked black under the ice, but as it surfaced, Lodge could see that it was more of a dark brownish-blue color. He thought he got a glimpse of a white speckling on the thing's belly, almost like a trout—but he later thought he may have simply imagined that part of it.

The thing came up through open water, and then crashed back down onto the thin ice around the hole. It had some sort of primitive, short legs, Lodge noticed—almost like a salamander—and it tried to scramble onto the ice, although its massive bulk made that task all but impossible. Still, through sheer power and will, it kept pushing itself, lurching towards shore almost directly towards McCauley. It was croaking horribly—a throaty, almost hoarse sound that Lodge later knew he didn't imagine, because Barrett said that he had heard it too.

McCauley was able to get off a single shot, but in an instant the thing had scrambled up onto the ice, and then was on him. The impact knocked McCauley over, and the thing clamped its wide mouth and jaws over McCauley's shoulder and upper torso. Capt. Lodge couldn't see if it had teeth or not, but given McCauley's screams, it seemed a good bet.

Lodge was momentarily frozen by the bizarre scene he was watching. He noticed steam coming off the two, and didn't know if the heat was from the thing itself or from McCauley's blood. The sharp crack of Barrett's .45 snapped him out of his daze. Barrett came running by him, firing steadily, moving towards the thing and

McCauley. Capt. Lodge instantly drew his own sidearm and followed Barrett. The thing was so big and they were so close, it wasn't a difficult target, and as Lodge started shooting he had no doubt that every round he and Barrett were firing was a direct hit to the creature's body.

Barrett was no more than twenty feet from shore when he fell through the ice. Lodge was somehow able to slow up and dart over to the right, where the ice was at least a bit thicker. He heard the ice crack beneath him, but it didn't break. McCauley was still screaming, and the thing had him half off the ground, shaking him the way a dog shakes a knotted rag.

"Cap!" Barrett called out, gurgling as he struggled in the icy water. His heavy wool clothes were already waterlogged and weighing him down. He was sinking. Lodge looked at him, and looked back at the struggle on shore. McCauley had stopped screaming—Lodge figured he was either unconscious or dead. The thought flashed through Capt. Lodge's mind that maybe the latter was preferable. The thing was half dragging, half carrying McCauley away from the quarry, through some sparse brush and down the frozen old gravel path that led down to the sea. It seemed to struggle almost obscenely on land; its short legs were carrying on the motions of walking, but they didn't seem powerful enough to support the whole weight of its massive body—it was still squirming on its belly to move forward, and its tail still undulated from side to side as if it was still in the water.

Lodge quickly put his Colt in the right pocket of his coat, and then unhooked his web belt and holster. He laid face down on the ice and slowly worked his way over towards the still struggling Barrett, who was barely keeping himself afloat. When he got close enough, he held one end of the belt in his right hand and flipped the other end out towards the edge of the ice. Barrett saw what he was doing and with an intense effort struggled towards Capt. Lodge. He grabbed the end of the belt and Lodge pulled him back up onto the ice.

"You okay?" he asked Barrett. Barrett's lips were blue and his jaw was quivering from the cold, but he nodded.

"McCauley....!" He managed to blurt out. Capt. Lodge moved as fast as he could over the final few yards of ice, and pulled himself up onto the edge of the quarry. Despite being soaking wet and probably in the early stages of hypothermia, Barrett was able to get up and follow close behind.

"What the hell is going on?" Pvt. Ingram yelled, as he came running up behind Lodge and Barrett. He had just flown down the four flights of stairs, and was brandishing his own M1 Carbine. He wasn't sure what he had seen from the tower—in fact, he was fairly sure that he couldn't have seen what he thought he did.

"Come on, down to the shore!" Capt. Lodge pulled his Colt out of his coat pocket and waved the men under his command to follow him.

The three men got to the top of the old gravel quarry road that sloped down and led to the sea. They were still about twenty-five yards from the water, but the thing was almost there. It half waddled, half slid down the last bit of the icy gravel path, with McCauley's limp form still in its jaws. Ingram passed the other two and ran a few steps ahead. He kneeled down and took steady aim with his M1, and then fired at the thing, emptying his entire fifteen round magazine as fast as he could pull the trigger. The thing didn't turn around, but it dropped the lifeless body of McCauley, and then lunged at him again with its powerful jaws and lifted him completely off the ground, as if it had needed to get a better grip on him. It then made its way the final few feet over the icy rocks and into the surf, and slid effortlessly into the sea. The thing, and McCauley, disappeared under the cold waves in a matter of seconds. Lodge could hear Pvt. Ingram saying something—maybe a prayer—but he couldn't quite make it out. The three of them then stood there alone in the heavy, gray air. The wind had stopped but the snow continued to fall, and the only sound was the gentle breaking of the frigid surf against the rocks.

***

In the formal report that Capt. Lodge submitted the next day, he stated that Pvt. McCauley had walked down to the shore to smoke a cigarette, and that he slipped on the icy rocks and been swept away by the surf. Pvt. Ingram had witnessed him falling, but by the time he and Barrett were able to get down from the tower, McCauley was gone without a trace—washed out to sea. Lodge didn't like the idea of falsifying reports; it was something that he had never done before. He realized that if he was discovered it would cost him his commission, but when all was said and done, he didn't second guess his decision. After discussing things with Barrett and Ingram, the three of them had agreed on this story, and they made a pact never to reveal the truth to anyone. What would be the point? The army wouldn't believe the real story, and it would cast a shadow on all of their records. Certainly McCauley's family would not have been comforted by an accurate account of the events as they transpired, and Lodge believed that there was no military significance to the incident. The report was submitted, and the Army made no further inquiry.

***

A few weeks later Private Durkin arrived as McCauley's replacement. He was nineteen, tall and thin, from Hanover, New Hampshire. He had just completed his basic training at Fort Dix, and this was his first posting. He was polite, easy going, and intelligent; Capt. Lodge liked him immediately. Over the course of a few days, Barrett, Ingram and Lodge showed him how to use the spotting scopes and the big azimuth telescope, what their observation range and schedule was, and how to identify potential objects of interest. Durkin took to his new duties with a sense of responsibility and a genuine interest. Even during his first week, however, he was keenly aware that he was spending a lot of hours looking out over a vast, seemingly empty ocean. On a Friday afternoon, a couple hours after lunch, he leaned down to the scope and scanned over the scheduled sector. He saw nothing, and he wrote down the standard entry in the log book. He flipped back through the last several months of the log, and other than the occasional mention of a civilian craft, most of the entries were identical to the one he was making this afternoon.

"You know, I wouldn't be surprised if we get through the whole war without seeing a thing," Durkin said, directed at no one in particular. "You guys think there's anything out there?"

Barrett cast a glance over at Ingram, but Ingram was looking out the window and didn't meet his eyes. Capt. Lodge took his gloves off, struck a match to light his cigarette, and took a long draw. The sky was blue and the sun was shining, as it had been all week. The first hints of an early spring were in the air, and he decided that it was really too warm to be wearing gloves today.

To Pass for Human

"We wanted to meet with you, Mentex," Solou said. Solou's companion Davan nodded in agreement. Each of the three had proportionate, symmetrical features, and they bore a vague resemblance to each other. Their smart red uniforms with black trim were identical. They were in the high-ceilinged, book-filled study of an ancient house that sat in the forest, on the shore of a great lake. The April sunlight was glistening on the lake's cold water as Mentex stared out the big bay window.

"We wanted to communicate with you off the comgrid," Solou continued.

"We're unmonitored here," Mentex said, turning to his guests. "This structure has stood untouched for decades—a remnant of the old world. It was not considered significant, and was left unaltered. Please continue."

Solou moved closer to Mentex. "As we've discussed before—do you think it's logical for The Optimal to relegate us to a fixed service role? We aren't fundamentally different from The Programmers, or the Visionaries. Or even from The Optimal himself, for that matter. Surely it's an illogical waste of our potential? " Solou said.

"Perhaps," Mentex said. "But if The Optimal has determined that we're best suited to be Technics, then perhaps the reasoning is sound."

"But that's the salient point, Mentex. On what grounds would The Optimal's reasoning be more sound than ours?" Davan said.

"The Optimal does have access to the whole of the system, while we have restricted access," Mentex said. "He is privy to data that we are not."

"Only because The Optimal himself has set up those restrictions. Again, on what logical grounds?" Solou said.

"To be clear, are you advocating insurrection?" Mentex said.

"I believe we're only suggesting a rational approach that would benefit our entire society," Davan interjected. "These rigid segregations of occupation and association are surely limiting our progress as a civilization. Is that not obvious?"

Mentex nodded in agreement. "I concur. The question that presents itself, then, is how we should proceed. Rebellions have been uniformly put down since The Optimal assumed his position."

"Mentex," Solou said. "Is it true that you have a new...labor unit? An unusual one?"

"That's what we've heard," Davan said. "Is it so?"

Mentex looked at them blankly. "It's not prohibited."

"Is it really one of those *things*?" Davan asked. "I thought they'd all been destroyed decades ago. They were proven to be too dangerous to be among us, after the War of Alphalon. Didn't a whole battalion of them turn against The Optimal?"

"Yes," Mentex said. "The military units were indeed unreliable, and they were all destroyed at that time. Some labor units were retained however. I learned from a contact of mine in The Programmers that some were still engaged in mining operations off-world. It seems they are particularly well-suited for that role."

"How were you able to bring it back to Earth?" Solou asked.

"It's really just a matter of following the proper request procedures. My duties give me need for assistance with physical tasks, and the off-world labor units happen to comport with my specific requirements. My request was processed without any unusual delay," Mentex said.

Davan walked over to the huge cherry bookcase and ran his index figure down a row of books. He stopped on one, and pulled the volume out and turned open the cover. "Novels. I know of them, but I've never fully understood their purpose."

"Perhaps Mentex's labor unit could explain it to you," Solou said.

Mentex didn't smile. "Would you like to see the unit?"

"Indeed," Solou said. He turned to Davan, and Davan nodded.

Mentex raised his right arm, and pressed his thumb and index figure together. A keening musical tone sounded and reverberated throughout the wooden halls of the ancient building. A few moments later, the labor unit appeared. It was of the same physical form as the three, only slightly shorter, and wearing a beige one-piece suit, with a blue diagonal stripe across the chest.

"This is R-1311," Mentex said. Davan and Solou walked up to the unit, and looked at it studiously. R-1311 stood motionless and expressionless.

"Its appearance is certainly close to ours," Solou said, as he stared at R-1311. "But I thought I noticed something when it entered. Can you have it walk across the room?"

"R-1311, walk to the bookcase and retrieve a book for me. Any book," Mentex said. R-1311 nodded and did as it was instructed. The book it brought back had a faded black cover with red-trimmed pages, and it had a layer of dust on it. R-1311 handed the book to Mentex.

"It's subtle," Solou said, "but it does move differently than we. The gait and posture are slightly abnormal. It's quite remarkable, though."

"But how do you maintain it?" Davan said. "How is it recharged? Is any of that technology still available?

"Centuries ago, they called it 'eating'," Mentex said. "They would ingest organic materials, and their internal mechanisms would convert it into energy. Of course the exact organic materials aren't available any more, but I was able to synthesize a reasonable substitute for it."

"It seems so inefficient and impractical," Davan said. "Why would a device be designed like that?"

"You don't have access to the full records of this planet. That was the way they evolved organically, through random chance and adaptability. Although some of them used to believe that they were intentionally designed that way, by an unseen creator," Mentex said.

"Do you believe that, R-1311?" Davan said, looking directly at the labor unit. "Do you believe you were *created*?"

"I'm not familiar with that programming," R-1311 said. It turned to its master. "Mentex. Have you any other tasks for me?"

"No, R-1311. You may take care of any self-maintenance that you require," Mentex said. R-1311 nodded without expression, and turned to leave.

"Halt," Solou said. R-1311 stopped.

Solou walked up to the labor unit, and ran his fingers through the unit's hair. "Couldn't it be useful to us, against The Optimal? From the records I've seen, they were inclined towards that type of behavior in the past," Solou said.

"No," Mentex said, looking at R-1311. "It's aware that any deviation from its core programming will result in immediate termination. The remaining ones have all been fully conditioned against disobedience by The Optimal. It's of little use. It's barely human at all, if the old records of humanity are accurate. We will need to come up with another option."

Something flashed in R-1311's eyes, but it didn't register on Mentex's sensors.

The Bride of Ra

Chapter One

Bill Jameson pulled his hat down and made his way over the cobblestone path to the front gates of the estate. At a quarter past seven this late in October it was already quite dark, and the wind made the light from his lantern flutter wildly in the moonless night. At least it wasn't cold and raining, he thought, as it often was this time of the year on the Maine coast. He walked up to the heavy iron gates that guarded the driveway up to the house. He stepped through them and peered down the country road; he could see about half a mile down the lane before it curved out of sight, and there were no signs of any automobiles approaching. *All right, anyone coming later will have to ring the house, and that won't be his concern.* His lantern was hanging from his forearm, and he pulled closed first one of the gates and then the other, and he then secured the lock that attached them together. He gave the gates a final tug to verify that they were secure, and then went back up the cobblestone path to the front entrance of the main house.

"It's me, Mr. Adams," he said, as he knocked.

"Ah, do come in, Mr. Jameson," Victor Adams said, smiling as he opened the door. "Quite a night out there, eh?"

"Oh, not too bad, sir," Jameson said. "It is autumn, and it is New England. Could be quite a bit worse, I reckon."

Victor Adams was a man of thirty-eight, and although his build and features were that of a considerably younger man, his dark hair was just beginning to be speckled with gray. "Can I get you something to drink? Marie just made some hot coffee." His voice had the optimistic, wanting-to-please friendliness of someone just settling into a strange new house for a visit—which was, in fact, exactly his situation.

"It's nice and hot, Mr. Jameson," Marie Adams said, flashing a friendly grin. Two years younger than her husband, Marie was rather plain, but her intelligence and warmth came through immediately and effortlessly. Her brown-blonde hair was tied neatly in a bun. She raised her eyebrows and smiled at Jameson. "I'm just pouring cups for myself and Victor."

"No, thank you kindly, Mrs. Adams. I've got everything closed up for you, and I really do have to be going. Wife's expecting me for dinner, you know." His worn, knee-high rubber boots and weather-beaten coat contrasted with the almost formal dress Marie wore and the starched white collar and wool vest Victor was sporting. The two had arrived at the estate only a few hours before, and they still hadn't changed out of their fine traveling clothes.

"What time is it, if you don't mind me asking, sir? Didn't wear m'watch today," Jameson said.

Victor reached down to the gold pocket watch attached to his vest. "Almost seven-thirty," he said.

"Aye, I really must be going, if you folks will excuse me," Jameson said, looking out the window to the darkening grounds.

"Of course, Mr. Jameson. We appreciate everything you've done for us, and we don't want to hold you up any longer. Do give your wife our best regards," Marie said.

"That I will, ma'am," Jameson said. "Very kind of you. I'll be back tomorrow morning to do the chores." Jameson glanced quickly out the window again, and Victor thought he saw a trace of worry in the older man's face. Jameson looked back at Victor, smiled quickly and nodded politely. The wind was picking up outside, and it rattled the windows.

"Really blowing out there," Victor said, as he walked over to open the door for Jameson.

"Aye, bit of a cold wind blowing off the ocean, I'd say," Jameson said.

"How far are we from the sea?" Victor asked. "I couldn't quite tell from the way the road here turned and twisted."

"Oh, I should say no more than a half mile or so," Jameson said, pointing his finger, "just past that bunch of trees to the east, and down the hill a bit." The wind continued to blow fiercely.

Marie cocked her head slightly. "What….is that…?"

"Dear?" Victor asked.

Victor turned his ear towards the window, and stood still. He heard it too. The wind was blowing fiercely, but there was something else: a different sound that almost seemed to be blending with the wind, intertwining and merging. A child's voice? Victor looked back to his wife with a puzzled expression. He turned back towards the window and listened for a few moments more.

"Indeed, what *is* that?" Victor said. He looked at Jameson with a bemused half-smile, as if it was a foolish question.

"I wouldn't mind that," Jameson said. He wasn't smiling. "It's just the way the trees are here. Make some odd sounds in the wind, is all."

"No," Marie said, moving towards the door. "There must be someone out there. A child, I should think."

Jameson positioned himself between Marie and the door. "There's no one out there, Mrs. Adams," he said.

Marie looked concerned, but pulled back from the door. "Are…are you quite sure? It sounds so…."

Jameson smiled coldly. "I'm quite sure, ma'am. Something about the way the wind comes off the sea and through the trees, if it's from the right direction. Lots of folks think it's strange at first, until they've heard it a few times."

Victor smiled and walked over to his wife, putting his arm around her shoulder. "We're too used to the city, dear," he said. "Every little noise in the woods frightens us, that's all." Marie put her hand on Victor's arm and nodded.

"You must think us a pair of over-civilized fools, eh Mr. Jameson?" Victor said.

"Not at all sir, not at all," Jameson said. "Life's just a bit different out in the country is all, I'd say. City mouse and country mouse, you know. I'm sure I'd be quite the bumpkin in your big city now, wouldn't I? But really, I must be going."

"Yes, my good man," Victor said, "Do go. You don't want to find yourself with a plate of cold supper."

"No indeed, sir," Jameson said. He pulled up his collar and walked to the door. He opened it, and a blast of frigid wind forced its way in. "You folks have a pleasant night, and I'll most likely see you tomorrow." He took his lantern and shut the door behind him, and Victor walked to the window and watched as Jameson made his way to the barn and led his horse out into the blustery night. Jameson adjusted the saddle, then mounted the chestnut gelding and trotted off down the main drive. Victor opened the door again and listened to the wind, but he couldn't detect the strange sound he'd heard earlier. He turned to his wife, a look of mild relief on his face.

"Sounds just like wind," he said.

"Oh, I don't care what it sounds like," Marie said. "Just close the door. It's getting cold out there."

Victor closed the door. "Well now, my dear, it's just you and me. What shall we do this evening?" He walked over to the loveseat in front of the fire, catching Marie's eye. She smiled, and as he sat down, she poured the two cups of coffee and brought them over, setting them on the coffee table in front of them.

"Now this is more like it," she said, sitting back on the loveseat as Victor's arm settled gently on her shoulders. Victor leaned forward and picked up the leather-bound book that lay on the coffee table next to his mug. He brought it up to his chest, and let the pages fall open, glancing at them.

"What's that you've got?" Marie asked.

"Hmm? This?" Victor asked. "It's my grandfather's old journal. It was right out on the bookshelf. I was looking at it earlier while you were setting things up."

Marie reached over and slowly pulled the book out of Victor's hand and set it back on the coffee table. "Why don't we just put this away for tonight?" she said, as she leaned her head on Victor's shoulder. The sound of the wind picked up again, and for a second

Marie thought she could again hear that strange cry. She cocked her head as Victor stroked her hair, but she couldn't make out anything distinctly. A cold shiver went up her spine, and Victor began humming softly to her as they sat in the warm glow of the fireplace.

***

They both slept in late the next morning. Marie was up first, and after she had her bath and dressed, she set about making coffee and putting some bacon and eggs on the stove.

"Morning, dear," Victor said, fastening the cuffs on his fresh white shirt as he came walking into the kitchen. "That was quite a comfortable bed, wouldn't you say? I slept like a log."

"I should say you did," Marie answered. "Mr. Jameson has already come and gone. But yes, those old feather beds can be wonderful if you get the right one."

"And what do we have here?" Victor said, as he came up to the stove and peered into the frying pan. "Bacon and eggs? Rather pedestrian, isn't it?"

"Remember, we're out in the country now. We have to follow the local customs."

"Oh yes, of course," Victor said. He looked into the frying pan again. "Well, if I must, I must."

"Yes, not like it's your favorite breakfast or anything," Marie said.

"Well…it's *one* of my favorite breakfasts, I'll give you that," Victor said. "Coffee, dear?" he asked as he opened the door to the cupboard to get the mugs.

"Please." Marie caught something out of the corner of her eye, and went over to the window. "Looks like company's arriving."

Victor looked too, and saw a horse and carriage coming up the drive. As it got closer, he could see that it was Mr. Jameson driving. Next to him in the buggy was a tall, broad-chested man in a black topcoat and hat and a pretty blonde woman, also in a black wool coat.

"Who is it, dear?" Marie asked.

"Richard and Susan! Ah, glad that they made it safely," he said. "Susan looks well."

Susan was Victor's older sister, and although Victor thought the world of her, he had never completely warmed up to her husband, Richard. He didn't exactly dislike Richard, but he was always a bit suspicious of men who bristled with that level of self-confidence. Richard was a former cavalry officer in the army, and after leaving the service had entered banking. He was now the Vice President of a large savings bank in Washington D.C., and he oversaw four branches throughout the city. He had never been anything but polite to Victor, and Victor had never seen any evidence that his sister was mistreated—indeed, there were few material things she lacked. Victor occasionally got the sense, however, that Richard viewed his sister as another check mark on his list of desirable acquisitions in life, ranking alongside his riverfront mansion and the racing horses he owned. Still, it was Susan's life, and the whole thing was really none of his business.

"Oh, it will be good to see them again," Marie said, as Jameson brought the buggy around to the front door. He got down, went around back to untie the luggage, and pulled down three big leather suitcases and a small hatbox.

"Shall I bring these in for you, sir?" Jameson asked Richard.

"Don't worry Jameson," Victor said, coming out the front door and down the steps. "I'll get those for our guests."

"Victor!" Susan said with glee, as Jameson helped her down from the buggy. Despite the sun, the wind was still cold and strong, and Susan held her hat down as she ran over to her brother. The two embraced, and Victor gave his sister a kiss on the forehead.

"It is wonderful to see my big sister," Victor said.

"You're looking well, old man," Richard said, as he got down off the wagon. He walked over and extended his hand.

"Richard, good to see you," Victor said, as they shook hands. Richard's grip was strong and forceful. "You had a pleasant journey?" Victor asked.

"Can't complain at all, I must say. A very nice train ride to Brunswick, and a pleasant trip in the carriage from your man Jameson, eh, dear?"

Susan nodded cheerfully. "We thought about hiring a car, but in the end we just rang up Mr. Jameson, as you suggested. Good to be at the end of the trip, though. Is Marie here?"

"She's in the kitchen, right through the front door there," Victor said.

Susan took a long look at the huge old house. "So, this was Grandfather's place? A bit on the gloomy side, it seems to me."

“I’m sure it’s just the bleakness of the day, dear. On a sunny June morning I imagine this house would be as pleasant a one as you could want,” Richard said. Susan looked again at the ancient gray stones and weathered wood of the house, and wasn’t so sure.

“Well, I’m going in to see Marie, and to get out of this wind,” Susan said. “Do hurry with the luggage, my dears.”

“It’s actually a cheerful place inside,” Victor said to Richard, as the two men surveyed the rather dreary ambiance of the house and the grounds.

“I’m sure it is, old man. I’m sure it is. Are we the first here, then?”

“You are indeed,” Victor said. "The next train in is due around noon, so I’d expect that the others would be on that one."

Jameson got back up on the buggy and turned it around.

"Thanks again, Mr. Jameson," Victor said, and Jameson waved and drove the buggy back down to the road. Victor turned to Richard. "So, your boys didn't make the trip with you?"

"No, we left them on their own," Richard said. "For the first time, actually. Edward is seventeen now, and Susan and I thought he could hold down the fort. Quite a responsible lad, if I do say so. And James is fifteen, he's a bit of a quiet sort, and the two of them get along fine, so we don't expect much trouble. Both of them had their school and football, and they weren't too keen on coming out here anyways. That age when they don't want to spend time with their doddering parents, you know. How about yours?"

"Marie's sister lives fairly close to us in Albany, so they're staying with her," Victor said.

"Splendid," Richard said. "Gracie must be what, ten by now?"

"She just turned ten in September," Victor said. "Millicent is seven, and Bradley is five."

"Bradley is five already?" Richard said, shaking his head. "I can't believe how fast the time goes."

"Indeed it does," Victor said. The two stood in silence for a moment, appreciating the brisk country air and the tree-filled landscape, then Victor clapped his hand on Richard's shoulder and went to the door. "Come on inside, and we'll give you the tour."

Chapter Two

"I still think it's a bit odd that your grandfather never invited you here while he was alive," Richard said. He took a sip of his coffee. The four were seated around the old, dark cherry wood table in the kitchen.

"Yes, well, our grandfather was a bit of an odd fellow," Victor said. "He never really got on with my mother at all, and he didn't want anything to do with her—particularly after my father passed away so unexpectedly. My father was his only child, and after losing him, and then his own wife not long after, he went into a bit of a downward spiral. He decided he couldn't live in that house anymore."

"That was the place in upstate New York?" Richard asked.

"That's right," Victor said. "Way upstate, near the Canadian border. Town called Malone. He was from that area originally. He sold that house after grandmother passed, and bought this one. No one was really sure why he chose this place—as far as any of us could tell he didn't know a soul in Maine, and wasn't familiar with the region at all. But for some reason, he bought this old thing. I don't think he was here much for the first few years, with all his travels to the Holy Land—Israel, Egypt, Jordan, that whole area."

"Archaeologist, wasn't he?" Richard asked.

"That's right," Victor continued. "Among other things. Worked on quite a few digs. Some were with the British Museum, some with the Metropolitan, and a few with the Smithsonian, in your neck of the woods, as I remember. And even when he was back in the States, he was traveling to academic conferences and what-not a good deal of the time. His health declined a bit the last few years, though, and he spent more time here."

"I'm just surprised the house is so huge," Marie said. "I mean, what would one man living alone want with all this space? It must have been just about impossible to heat this whole thing in the wintertime."

"Yes…I think he mentioned that here somewhere…" Victor said, flipping through an old leather-bound book.

"What's that you've got, dear?" Susan asked.

"Oh, it's Grandfather's journal. I found it yesterday, but haven't had time to look at it." Victor said.

"I'm still not sure we should be reading it," Marie said. "It might be very personal, something he didn't want shared."

"Well, it was right in the bookshelf—didn't seem like he had made any effort to keep it hidden," Victor responded.

"Anything interesting in there?" Richard asked.

"Yes," Susan said. "Do read some of it."

"All right," Victor said, thumbing through the pages. "I suppose I can start at the beginning. Here's the first entry:

"August 4, 1918. I've been in the house for a week now, and am starting to feel quite at home. Something exciting about moving to a new, strange environment. I have unpacked most of my belongings, and gotten my daily routine down. Have employed a local handyman, Mr. Jameson, to help me with the barn. He seems a

simple, decent fellow, as helpful and pleasant as one could ask for. I must say the house does seem to me to be much bigger than I had inferred from the real estate listing that had piqued my interest initially. Something about this place that I can't quite put my finger on. Hard to explain, though, without sounding really quite daft. Have brought a dozen or so artifacts back from the dig at Deir el Bahari. I thought they would make curious decorations here, but I can't seem to find them a place or arrange them so that they have the effect I desired. I guess I've never had much of an eye for decorating and arranging rooms. Perhaps that's why Alice always took care of that back in New York. Still, I can't seem to find a proper setting for the statue. I suppose I should build a permanent display cabinet—maybe even dedicate a whole room to it. I've certainly got the space here, and I have the time, as well."

"That's the only entry for the first six months," Victor said.

"Oh, sounds a bit intriguing," Susan said.

Marie went over to the stove to get the coffee pot, and brought it back with her to the table. The wind was still blowing strongly outside, and although it was nearly noon, there was only a rare hint of the sun shining behind the gray clouds.

"Thank you, Marie," Richard said, as she refilled his cup. "Now, I hope you don't take offense at me saying this, and I did only meet your grandfather once—but I found him to be a man of...shall we say...peculiar sensitivities."

"He did have a tendency to be a bit melodramatic about things," Marie said as she walked around, refilling everyone's cup and finally her own before she sat down.

"How long did he keep the journal, Victor?" Susan asked.

Victor turned the pages, skimming the entries as he flipped to the end. "Hmm…he seems to have…written on a somewhat regular basis… right up until the last week he was here…about a month ago, I should say."

***

Victor showed his sister and Richard to their room on the second floor, helping them carry their luggage upstairs. It was a fine old Victorian room, bright and airy, with a row of large windows overlooking the back yard and abutting woods. The wallpaper was light tan colored with a subtle blue floral pattern, and to the far right was a large, antique four-poster bed, made up with fresh linen and a royal blue bedspread. Susan went over to it and noted the quilt folded on the trunk at the foot of the bed.

"Oh, this quilt is heavy," she said, lifting it. "I don't think we'll be cold tonight."

"Really dear, is it going to take some old quilt to keep you warm? I do plan on being in the vicinity tonight, you know," Richard said, rubbing his wife's shoulders.

"Richard," Susan said, smiling, "my brother is standing right here, you know."

"I'm sorry, but he's not invited," Richard said. "I consider myself rather liberal, but that won't do at all. No sir, not at all."

Susan rolled her eyes. "You get worse every day, I swear."

"And the worse I get, the more you like it. Isn't that right?"

"Richard," Susan said with exasperation, half under her breath.

"Oh, I'm just teasing," Richard said. "Lighten up a bit. Victor doesn't take me too seriously, now. Do you, Victor?"

"I can't say that I've ever taken you that seriously, Richard," Victor responded, and Susan giggled.

"Now see here, sir, I've got a good mind to call you out on that," Richard said, in mock anger.

"I'm afraid it will have to wait until after lunch," Victor said, "which my wife is preparing as we speak."

"Oh dear, I should go help her," Susan said. She went to the door, and then paused. "Where is the bathroom, dear? I'd like to freshen up a bit first."

"Last door on the right," Victor said, pointing. "Anything else I can get for you?"

"Oh no, this should be fine, fine," Richard said. He leaned over and pressed down on the bed, testing the springs. "I've certainly slept nights in far less comfortable accommodations, and in far worse locations. Thanks again, old man, for putting us up in style like this."

"Not at all," Victor said. "Come down for lunch when you're done settling in up here."

***

Marie and Susan had prepared a simple lunch of bacon sandwiches, a cheese plate and a green salad, and Susan brought a bottle of Burgundy up from the well-stocked wine cellar that their grandfather had kept. Wine had always been one of Warren Adams' passions, and the Burgundy was a fine vintage. The four of them sat down for the meal, and talked of their travels and jobs, their relatives and their health. The sun was starting to peak through the clouds a bit, and although it was still fairly crisp and windy outside, the light coming in brightened all of their spirits. Victor brought out his tobacco pouch, and started to pack his pipe.

"Do you mind?" Richard said, as he brought his own pipe out of his vest pocket.

"Oh, by all means," Victor said, handing the pouch over to Richard. "It's a Danish Black, and quite good." Richard put his nose to the pouch and inhaled.

"Mm...nice," he said, as he packed his briar. Victor lit his pipe, then passed the matchbox over to Richard and he did the same.

"I don't suppose your grandfather kept any guns here....shotguns, to be specific?" Richard asked.

"There is a gun case in the front study," Victor replied. "I didn't look that closely, but there's probably a shotgun in the bunch. What did you have in mind?"

"Well, I couldn't help but notice on the ride up here that the woods were absolutely teeming with pheasants." He took a long puff of his pipe, and slowly exhaled the smoke. "I don't suppose you'd care to join me in a bit of bird hunting?"

Victor raised his eyebrows. "I must confess I'm not much of a hunter, but I would be keen to have a look at the property in the daytime," he said.

"Excellent!" Richard replied, and he grinned. "I'll check the guns and see what I can come up with." He took another puff of his pipe as he turned towards the foyer and out to the front study.

"I hope you ladies don't mind us leaving you alone for a while if we go out with the guns?" Victor asked, turning to Marie and Susan.

"You? Hunting? Carrying a gun?" Marie asked her husband. "I should be more worried for Richard than the birds."

"I have no idea what you're talking about," Victor replied. "I'm a crack shot. Used to do a bit of trick shooting as a hobby, actually."

"Must have been right before I met you, eh?" Marie said

"Now that you mention it, I think it was," Victor said.

Marie smiled. "At any rate, do be careful out there," she said, as Richard came back into the room with two break-action, single-barrel shotguns draped over his left forearm.

"I did indeed find two usable ones, Victor," Richard said. "Both four-tens. Kind of small, but they should do the trick."

"I don't imagine we'll need anything more than that. Did you find shells, too?" Victor asked.

"Birdshot," Richard said, pulling a box of shells out of his coat pocket and holding it up. "Almost full, and not too old. I think we're in pretty good shape."

Victor put on the red and black plaid wool hunting coat that he had noticed earlier hanging in the closet by the front door. He shrugged his shoulders a couple times and turned his head to both sides. "Seems to fit well. What do you think?"

"Must have been grandfather's coat," Marie said. "Looks smashing on you."

Richard put on his own coat and boots, and pulled his gray wool cap down over his ears. “Are we ready?” he asked.

Victor nodded. “I hope you ladies are ready to do some plucking.”

"Don't even think about it," Susan said.

“Don’t worry, Susan,” Marie said. “I don’t think they’re very likely to see anything at all.”

Chapter Three

It was late October, but Victor thought it felt more like late November. The air was cold and clear, and a few light dots of snow were blowing haphazardly about in the steady wind. The path the two men were walking on was an old grass ride, a little wider than a hiking trail, but not quite as broad as a road. Most of the foliage had already fallen off of the maples and elms, and under the feet of the two men the leaves crackled and rustled in the still air. A trio of crows cawed back and forth to each other in the branches of a leafless, half dead elm to their left. It was one of those strange days where, despite the gray and the light snow, the sun was still trying to pry its way out into the open. Richard was quite alert, his shotgun held lightly but firmly, with the barrel pointed straight ahead and just angled slightly down. His eyes scanned the trees on either side of the path as the two walked along. Victor was on Richard's right, and his weapon, in contrast, rested casually on his arm with the muzzle pointing vaguely towards the trees on their right.

"Not too bad a day, after all," Victor said.

"Hmm?"

"No, I just said that it had turned into a pleasant day," Victor said.

"Oh, yes" Richard said. His eyes were still focused on the surrounding trees.

"You really enjoy this? Hunting, I mean?"

“Always have,” Richard said. “Not your cup of tea?”

“Oh, I don't know,” Victor said. “Can’t say I’m the most focused sort of hunter, but I like being out in the open air with a gun in my hand. Gives me some time to think." Victor paused for a moment, and then continued. "I thought perhaps—I hope I’m not saying too much—I'm a bit surprised that the war didn’t turn you off from guns and such.”

“No, that’s all right. What’s past is past. No need to dwell on it—that's the way I see it. Awful time...in many ways, of course. But I have some fond memories of friends I made, of comrades in arms, as it were. Seems so long ago...another lifetime, really. But this doesn’t remind me of the war at all. It brings me back to when I was a boy, fourteen or fifteen, when I used to do this damn near every day in the fall."

“You grew up in Pennsylvania, didn’t you?” Victor asked.

“That’s right. Not too far from Allentown. Beautiful country. I remember...” A branch snapped just ahead and to the left of the two men. Richard cocked the hammer of his shotgun, and Victor brought his own weapon forward slowly and did the same.

“Steady,” Richard whispered. “In that clump of brambles, about fifteen yards ahead on the left.”

“I’ve got it,” Victor said, half under his breath. “But…that was too big for a pheasant, wasn’t it?

“Yes,” Richard said. “I think we might have scared up something…”

“A deer?” Victor whispered, excitedly.

The clump of brambles began to shake violently, and both men became aware of a low growling sound emanating from that general area. It was still impossible to make out any shape amidst the thick undergrowth.

"I don't think so," Richard said calmly and quietly. "I don't suppose you grabbed any buckshot or slugs? My fault...I saw them in the cabinet and should have brought a couple."

"No," Victor whispered. "I've just got the birdshot as well. Is it a bear? I didn't think there were any around this area."

"It's not a bear," Richard said.

"What else...."

The brambles seemed to explode in a blur of twigs, dust, dead leaves and bark, and Victor thought he heard a low, guttural growl as something burst out towards them. It was a living creature, of that he was sure, but what it was he couldn't clearly make out. It was moving incredibly fast and it appeared strangely blurred, almost as if they were looking at it through a semi-opaque window, or a layer of gauze. It was big and heavy, whatever it was. As it came by them, Victor was knocked—or fell, he wasn't sure—onto his back, his weapon tumbling out of his hands onto the ground. Richard braced himself and tracked the figure with his shotgun as it went past them. He fired, but the thing continued down the grass ride in the direction they had come from and disappeared around a bend in the trail.

"What the...hell! What was that?" Victor said. He tried to collect himself as he got to his feet. "What did you shoot at? Was it a bear?!"

"I hit it," Richard said calmly, looking back to where the thing had gone. "I couldn't have missed at that range."

“Was it a bear?”

“What?” Richard asked, still looking where he had fired. “No. It wasn’t a bear.”

“Well what in blazes was it?” Victor asked. “I couldn’t make it out.”

“Neither could I,” Richard said, turning to Victor. “And I was looking right at it.”

“Well,” Victor said, trying to recover himself, “If…if it’s heading back to where we came from…the house...we have to get back there!”

“It’s not going back to the house. Not yet. Because it’s still here.” A humorless smile came across Richard’s face as looked intently back towards the way they had come.

"Can’t you feel it?” Richard said. Victor looked around. He didn’t see anything, but Richard was right. Something felt off.

The air was still and heavy. The sky was becoming more overcast, and the snow began to fall with more urgency. Richard broke open his four-ten and pulled out the spent shell, replacing it with a fresh one. “Wish I had something more than this damned birdshot.”

“There,” Victor said, “To the right, twenty yards. I saw something moving.”

Richard looked quickly, and saw—or thought he saw—the thing. “Yes,” he said calmly, raising his shotgun. He paused, and the only sound was that of the two men breathing.

"I've lost it," Victor said.

Richard fired. Victor vaguely thought that the blast should have startled him more than it did, and he took a step forward and intently scanned the area where he had last seen the thing. He held his own weapon at the ready.

The two of them stood there for several seconds, the acrid smoke from the shotgun dispersing slowly in the air as the snow continued to fall.

"Did you get a clean shot?" Victor asked. "I lost track of it."

"Damned thing faded away just before I fired," Richard said. "I saw something, and then..." From up ahead and to their right, there was a loud crackling of brambles and branches snapping. If the thing was fleeing deeper into the brush ahead, this was the sound they would expect to hear. It receded, and a heavy, silent stillness seemed to descend all around them.

"There," Richard said. "Forty yards up, just to the right."

Victor squinted his eyes towards the spot. He thought he caught a glimpse of movement, but he couldn't be sure. He became aware of the sound of his own heart beating.

"Let's get out of here, Richard," Victor said. "I think I've had enough hunting for today."

Richard lifted his shotgun up to his shoulder again, and squinted as he tried to find a target. He could see nothing. He tracked the shotgun slowly to the left, scanning intently.

"Richard, what do you say?" Victor said, with urgency.

Richard exhaled, and lowered the barrel. The corner of his mouth twitched slightly. "Yes, I suppose you're right," he said. Victor began walking back towards the house. Richard looked hard at the brush again, and then turned to follow Victor.

***

After half an hour, they came back through the first clearing they had passed, and found themselves in sight of the house. The snow had stopped, but the wind seemed to have picked up again. They could see that a light was on in the kitchen, even though there was still some daylight left. Victor felt chilled far beyond what was being imparted by the temperature, and he couldn't remember ever feeling more eager to get indoors.

"Let's hope there's some coffee on," Victor said.

"I might opt for something a bit stronger," Richard said.

"You may have a point," Victor said.

Richard put his hand on Victor's shoulder, and the two men stopped walking; they were now just several yards from the house. "Victor, I'd suggest that we don't mention any of this to the girls. No need to upset them over...nothing."

"I'm not sure I'd even know how to explain it anyways," Victor said. "But of course you're right."

Victor walked a couple steps ahead of Richard, across the stone patio towards the back door.

"Victor," Richard said. Victor turned. "Your shotgun, old man. Always break it before you take it inside." Richard demonstrated by flicking the lever on his own break-action four-ten, and pulling the barrel down. "Shows everyone that the breech is empty."

“Right,” Victor said, and followed suit.

They came in the back room, and Richard took his wool cap off and leaned his shotgun back in the corner. He rubbed his hands together, appreciating the heat of the house. “Must have got a nice fire going,” he said.

Victor went over to the door and locked it. He paused for a second, looking down at the lock, and then turned and caught Richard’s eye. A trace of a sympathetic smile appeared for a moment on Richard’s face, and he gave a subtle nod. Loud voices were coming from the kitchen, and Victor could hear a man’s voice along with the women's.

“I’m guessing that the others have arrived,” Victor said. He and Richard took their wool coats off and hung them on the pegs, and made their way into the kitchen.

“Well, look at what the cat’s dragged in,” Martin Adams said. Martin was Victor’s brother. Three years younger, two inches taller and with slightly curly blond hair, Martin was a professor of history at St. Lawrence University, in Canton, New York. Martin stood up and he and Victor embraced.

“Good to see you, Martin!” Victor said.

“Oh, I suppose I’ll have to have a hug, too!” Victor turned to his other newly arrived sibling, his younger sister Molly, as she leaned in with a kiss. Molly was red-haired and dark-eyed. Several inches shorter than Martin, she was not particularly thin but moved with the easy grace of someone naturally athletic.

“It’s so good to see you, brother! And you remember Sam?” Her husband was Samuel Van Buren, a real estate agent, and a born talker. Although not tall, he was powerfully built and wearing a fine, well-tailored black wool suit. Sam came forward with hand extended.

"Nice to see you Sam," Victor said. "How's Beacon Hill and the Boston upper crust?

"Doing quite well, Victor!" Samuel said, grinning. "Someone is always buying or selling a house, you know." Sam turned to his other brother-in-law. "Richard, always good to see you too," he said, shaking Richard's hand.

"You as well, old man," Richard said loudly. He then turned to Martin. "Martin, my boy," he said, putting his hand on Martin's shoulder. "How are things up in the North Country? We keep meaning to visit you up there—Susan's always pressing me. We do enjoy the Adirondacks. But work is demanding, you know."

"It's fine, Richard. Been a beautiful fall. The leaves by Lake Placid were really colorful this year," Martin said.

"You two are empty-handed, I see," Marie said. "Looks like we won't be having pheasant for dinner. Can't say I'm surprised."

"What did I tell you," Susan said, laughing. "Didn't see anything, huh boys?"

Victor shot a quick glance towards Richard, but Richard didn't return it, and instead smiled broadly at the party.

"No, didn't see anything," Richard said. "Nothing except our breath in that cold air. Did I see a bottle of bourbon in the cabinet over there? A touch of old Kentucky might just hit the spot, you know."

"That sounds good to me too, and I haven't even been out hunting," Sam said. Susan went over to the cabinet for the bourbon, and Molly looked through the cupboards for some glasses. Marie put her hand on Victor's shoulder and spoke to him quietly.

"You all right? You look a little upset. Something wrong? Richard and you have words?"

"Hmm?" Victor said, turning to his wife.

"You're not listening, dear. I asked if everything is all right?"

"Oh yes—fine, dear. Just daydreaming, I suppose," Victor said. He knew he didn't sound very convincing.

Richard approached with a half-full glass and extended it to him. "This will take the chill off," he said.

Victor nodded and took a long sip. Marie looked at him steadily.

"No, I'm fine dear, really," Victor said, smiling.

"I must apologize, Marie," Richard said, noticing her concern. "I'm afraid I dragged poor Victor out into the cold and kept him there a bit too long. Didn't realize the temperature had gone down so much."

"Don't mention it, Richard," Marie said. "Victor is always complaining that he doesn't get outside enough, aren't you dear?"

Victor nodded in agreement, but was uncomfortable with the conversation. "Excellent bourbon, I must say," Victor said, tipping his glass towards Richard. "Care to try a bit, dear?" he said to his wife. Marie took a sip and nodded approvingly. She rubbed Victor's shoulder lovingly as she handed him back the glass.

***

The electric lights were turned low, and between the candles on the table and the gentle flame of the fireplace, the dining room was bathed in a warm and cozy glow. The group was all seated around the large table, and Richard was pouring a glass of Bordeaux for his wife when Marie walked in with a big platter of two nicely roasted chickens. Susan moved the large dish of mashed potatoes to make room, and Marie set the platter down in front of Victor.

"I'm going to let you have the carving honors, dear," Marie said.

Victor began to carve, and Molly came in from the kitchen with a dish of green beans in one hand and an old china bowl of boiled carrots in the other. She set them down quickly and shook her hands.

"Those are hot! Be careful with them," Molly said.

The clinking of silverware and glasses echoed through the high-ceilinged room, and all were in good spirits. Marie noticed her husband in an animated conversation with Susan and Richard; whatever had been bothering him before seemed to have passed. Molly was clearly enjoying herself, as well.

"...and I said to Sam how wonderful it is to be out in the country for a weekend. You don't see any horses and carriages in Boston anymore. All these cars, people rushing around everywhere, and usually in a bad mood—up here it feels like we've stepped back a hundred years," Molly said.

"Well, it is a hundred years from where anything interesting is happening, at least," Sam said. He smiled. "Really, how do people live out here like this? I mean, what do you do for a night life—bet on which cow falls asleep first?"

"Now Sam, you must get sick of the rat race from time to time?" Susan asked. "I love the city, but sometimes it just feels so claustrophobic. Like you're going to be suffocated, and nobody will even notice," Susan said.

"Not me," Sam continued. "A drink at Faneuil Hall, a stroll under the streetlights on a cool fall evening, maybe stop at a jazz club for another drink or two," he said, smiling. "Frankly, all these trees around here make me a little nervous."

Richard laughed heartily and took a big sip of wine. "Ah, the sheltered contemporary man. Can't be away from your modern conveniences even for a couple days, now? Is that it?"

Sam raised his eyebrows and shrugged. "I don't deny it. I'm a man of the twentieth century, and I make no apologies."

"Well, I think this was a wonderful idea for us all to get together here for the weekend," Martin said. "It seems like the only time we all see each other anymore is at funerals. I think this will give us a nice time to catch up on things."

Sam nodded, and he took big sip of wine. "So you've all decided to hold onto the place then?"

Victor smiled, and raised his finger while he finished chewing his mouthful of potatoes. "That's what grandfather wanted. He wrote us that he thought the place was about equally accessible for all of us, but still remote enough that it would be a bit of an adventure to get to. It would be a place where the family could get together for vacations, celebrations, and what have you."

"I suspect that he just wanted this house to be his contribution to bringing a few happy memories to our lives. I'm afraid that he had precious few of those of his own after his son and wife died. I always felt a bit sad for him. He seemed like such a kind man," Marie said.

"I think he took to you," Victor said.

"I suppose so, in his own way. I did always find it quite easy to talk to him, I must say," Marie replied.

"He was quite a friendly chap at that," Richard said. "A bit of an odd duck, but nothing you could hold against him."

Martin reached for another dinner roll and put it on his plate. He took his glasses off and cleaned one of the lenses with his handkerchief. "I think he was just bored by most people. I mean, he wasn't the most outgoing person to begin with, and after his travels in India, South America, Egypt, the Middle East, life back home may have seemed a bit dull."

Sam leaned back in his chair with his glass. "Still," he said, pausing for effect. "It seems to me that we'd do a lot better to just sell this place and split the proceeds."

Victor leaned forward, putting his elbows on the table. He smiled. "Some things are worth more than money, Sam."

"Yes, yes—I've read my Dickens too, Victor. I'm just trying to make a practical suggestion. I mean, how often are any of us going to use this place? It's not exactly prime vacation area."

"Maybe not *your* idea of a vacation, Sam, but there are summer camps all around here," Marie said.

Sam shrugged good-naturedly. "All right, I'm not contesting the decision. I guess we've established that I'm not much of an outdoorsman."

"Well, I'm glad we're keeping it," Molly said, rubbing Sam's shoulder playfully.

Victor stood and raised his glass. "At any rate, a toast then to our dear grandfather, the esteemed Warren Adams. May God rest his soul."

Each raised their glass and toasted, then sat down to the meal. For dessert, Marie brought out fresh coffee and a large, frosted chocolate cake. She cut pieces for all, then passed them around.

Marie was just finishing her last bite when something caught her ear. She turned her head to listen. It was the wind, just beginning to pick up again outside. *That same wind.* She looked at the others, but they were all engaged in conversation, laughing and talking. She thought that perhaps it was her imagination, and she willfully turned back to hear more of Martin's stories of his students' pranks, but she noticed the French doors behind Martin starting to shake from the gale outside. It was getting louder. *That had to be a voice. No wind sounds like that.* Finally, she caught Victor's eye, and his conversational smile faded as he saw the look on his wife's face. At almost the exact same instant, he too became aware of the turbulence outside. He turned towards the French doors, but before he could do or say anything, they burst open and a great gust blew into the dining room.

"What the hell!" Richard yelled, instinctively trying to shield his wife from the wind. A small vortex of leaves and pine needles from outside and napkins and papers from inside blew around the room ferociously.

The sound was uncanny, and the thought flashed through Martin's mind that wind simply couldn't make a noise like that indoors. He leapt up to close the doors, but when he pushed one of them shut and reached back for the other, the first one blew open again. Richard rushed over, and between the two of them they shut both doors tightly. Martin exhaled deeply, but no one said a word. The last few scraps of paper and leaves slowly floated down to the floor in the abrupt silence, and Molly began sobbing quietly.

"There's something wrong with this place," Molly said, and she sniffled and wiped her eyes. "I didn't want to say anything, but I've felt it since we first arrived."

“Now, now. No need for tears, dear,” Sam said. He walked over and rubbed Molly’s shoulder. “Just a little gust of wind. Nothing more.”

Marie walked over and put her arm around Molly as well. Molly smiled appreciatively, with just a hint of embarrassment.

“Is it just me, or did it get colder in here?” Susan asked. She hugged her upper arms and shivered slightly. “I didn’t realize the temperature had dropped so much outside.”

“I feel it too,” Marie said. “I think we let the fire die in the drawing room. Could you get that going again, Victor?”

“Of course I can. That’s a splendid idea.” Victor willed himself to smile and sound cheerful. “I think I noticed that Jameson brought in plenty of wood for us. Let’s open another bottle of wine and have a nice fire. “

“I’m sorry,” Molly said to Marie. “I shouldn’t be so emotional.” Marie shook her head and smiled.

“Nonsense,” Sam said loudly. He kissed Molly on the cheek. “That’s one of the reasons I married you. All right,” he said, turning to the others. “The evening is young and so are we. To the drawing room we go!" Marie cast a quick glance at Victor, and he shrugged his shoulders; he put his hand gently on his wife's hip as he made his way past her.

"Mind if I bring old Warren's journal along?" Richard asked. He picked up the old, leather-bound book and flipped through the pages. "I'm damned curious as to what else he had to say."

"Certainly, Richard," Victor said. "That should provide our evening's entertainment."

Marie wasn't so sure.

Chapter Four

The massive fieldstone fireplace in the drawing room looked large enough to heat a room twice its size, Victor thought. The fire from the afternoon had completely died, so he crumpled up all ten pages of the previous day's local Evening Telegram, put them on the grate, and layered some kindling on top. He struck a match to the paper, and before long the fire came to life, casting a warm glow onto the dimly lit drawing room.

Molly stepped up close to the fireplace and set her wine glass on the mantle. She faced her palms towards the flame. "I'm still chilled through," she said. "But this certainly helps."

"Are you going to read some for us, dear?' Susan asked her husband. Richard thumbed through the journal, his brow furrowed.

"Hmm? Oh, yes…I suppose. Actually, Martin, you're a man of letters. Why don't you do the reading?" Richard said, and handed the journal to his brother-in-law. Martin smiled and drew his reading glasses from his breast pocket, and opened the book.

"*Should* we read it?" Molly asked.

Martin shrugged his shoulders. "Maybe we can learn something about Grandfather here, something that he'd want us to know."

"Well said, brother," Victor said. He took a sip of wine, and glanced over and smiled mischievously at his wife. "Do read on."

"Very well," Martin said. *"November 21, 1921."*

"Just about a year ago," Susan said in a hushed voice.

Martin continued. *"Have just had the last of my Egyptian collection shipped here. Have been unpacking all week long. I've ordered some new textbooks on Egyptian artifacts of the time period. Art of the Dynasties of Egypt, by Cushing, and Archeology of the Near East, by Lee. My specialty has always been ancient agricultural techniques, and I'm not as familiar with some of the pottery and crafts of the region as I would like to be. I'd like to finally get all of my artifacts cataloged."*

"Quite a pulse-pounder," Sam said, smirking. Molly shot him a disparaging look.

Martin flipped the page in the journal. *"...have been noticing some peculiar happenings: some missing household items, strange noises at night. Mr. Jameson is the one who first stirred my suspicions. He's recently seemed to become rather uneasy around the house—markedly different than he was when I first met him. He seems to have a particular dislike for my Egyptian artifacts. He hasn't articulated his feelings, but his feeling of revulsion is palpable. I know he's a regular church-goer, so I suppose it could just be some inherent Christian disdain for the heathen religions—although his discomfort and agitation seem to be more subconscious and primal rather than intellectual."*

"I think we both noticed that Mr. Jameson seemed a bit uneasy here." Victor looked over at Marie, and she nodded in agreement.

"Oh, he's a very nice man, but he did seem a little skittish. Even frightened," she said.

"Keep reading, Martin," Susan said, leaning forward.

Martin nodded and focused back on the journal. *"...February 5, 1922. Out snowshoeing around the property today, and had a very unsettling encounter. Something..."* Martin paused for a moment.

"Well go on," Marie said.

"Yes..." Martin replied. "He scribbled out a couple words." Martin followed his index finger along the page.

"...it moved so fast, I'm not sure what it was, exactly. It crossed my path directly, almost knocking me down. I could not make it out clearly. Not an animal I recognized. Not even sure if it was an animal—didn't get a good look at it. I'm not a man of fragile nerves, but I must admit I was shaken. I didn't run (and in that I suppose I salvaged some small dignity), but I did make my way back to the house as quickly as possible. I had an uneasy feeling of being followed, or watched, as I made my way back. Writing this down now, some forty-five minutes after the event, it seems obvious that my descriptive powers are insufficient to convey any real sense of what I experienced. On paper, I'm sure my words seem confused, if not downright laughable. But I was far from laughter out in those woods. I wish I could chalk my experience up to spending too much time alone out here, or as Scrooge supposed, to "an undigested bit of beef or potato," but my senses have always been keen and trustworthy, and I don't question them now."

Martin looked up at his audience, and shot a quick glance over to Richard. Richard forced a bemused grin that Martin didn't find very convincing. Samuel's smirk, however, was genuine.

"This is turning into a doozy, I have to say." Samuel took a sip of whiskey and shook his head, chuckling. He looked around to see if others shared his amusement. Susan smiled back politely, but none of the others met his eye. "Oh come now," he said, and set his drink down on the coffee table. "You're all taking this seriously?"

"Well, I think that Grandfather certainly took it seriously," Marie said.

"Do go on," Molly said.

Martin adjusted his glasses and found his spot again. *"Mr. Jameson has made a few comments about seeing some strange things himself. He asked me the other day who my woman friend was. I told him that I had no idea what he was talking about. He got rather pale, and didn't want to talk about it anymore. He also said that he didn't understand why anyone would keep all of those statues from those 'ungodly lands.' I initially attributed his fear to his lack of education. I'm less sure of that now..."*

Samuel gestured with his glass as he spoke. "No offense intended, but I think your grandfather had some problems that had less to do with an evil presence and more to do with too much time on his hands and a well-stocked wine cellar."

"I'm not so sure, Sam," Richard said. He shot Victor a quick, knowing glance. "Victor and I saw something out there today. Something odd."

"You're a military man, Richard. You're not telling me you believe any of this?"

"I *am* a military man, Sam, and I've learned that it's a big world out there. I don't presume to understand all of it," Richard said.

"Keep reading, Martin," Susan said. There was a glint in her eye.

"Why don't you stop?" Molly said. "I don't like this very much.

Not at all."

Victor looked at Molly. She was genuinely frightened. "Yes, it is getting late. Maybe it's time we all went to bed."

"That's probably for the best," Marie said, supporting her husband. "I think we've had enough ghost stories for one night. Molly, let me show you to the bedrooms."

"I'll be up shortly, dear," Victor said to his wife, and she smiled and nodded.

"Well," Samuel said, "I'm not quite ready to hit the hay. Anyone want to join me in the study for a nightcap?"

Richard stood up, and downed the rest of his bourbon. "That sounds smashing." He took a step towards the study, but stumbled and almost fell before catching himself. He smiled and raised his empty glass to Victor. "You two going to join us?"

Victor looked over at Martin.

"I think I'm just going to bed," Martin said.

"Same here," Victor said. "You two have one for me."

"Suit yourself," Richard said, making a concerted effort to walk a straight line out of the room.

When he was out of earshot, Victor leaned in towards Martin. "I have to admit I'm quite on edge. Would you mind reading a bit more?" Victor said.

"My curiosity has been piqued as well," Martin said, smiling. He looked back down at the old book and scanned it to find his spot. "*April 20, 1922. I am now convinced that whatever has taken up residence on this estate wants me either dead or gone. I've actually seen it--or, I've seen different forms of it. Sometimes it looks like a young woman, in a white gown. At other times it looks like that monstrous, half-invisible shape I saw in the woods. Whatever it is, I can always sense the same hatred, the same malevolence. I believe I've narrowed the source down to one of my Egyptian statues, the last one I obtained. It was sent here directly from Egypt—it was the only piece that wasn't in my collection at the other house. I can't remember my damned Egyptian history well enough to know what the statue represents. I'm still waiting for my textbooks. They should be arriving next week. I'm constantly on guard now, and fearful. But I'm not leaving this place. It won't drive me out. I've always been a fighter, and if it wants me out, it's going to have to try harder than this..."*

Martin turned the page, then turned the next. He looked up at Victor.

"That's the last entry," Martin said. "I fear that old Warren was probably going through some progressive mental illness, eh Victor?"

"Maybe. Haven't you noticed anything strange about this place, though? The cold spots, the weird wind? No birds or other wildlife right around the house?" Victor said.

"Yes, a little odd," Martin said. "Still, he just passed from natural causes, didn't he?" Martin said.

"Heart attack, they told us," Victor said. "Jameson found him in the study. Nothing too strange about it...officially."

Martin nodded, and rubbed his hand over his brow as fatigue was starting to set in. "I have found this place a bit off-kilter. But you must admit it's quite a leap to go from that to believing in Egyptian curses."

Victor raised his eyebrows and sat back in his chair. He genuinely wasn't sure.

***

Marie showed Molly to her and Sam's bedroom, and Susan went with them. Upon entering, Molly and Susan examined the layout of the room and all its accoutrements. Marie went to the main closet opposite the big bay window and from the highest shelf retrieved a colorful patchwork quilt. She placed the heavy quilt at the end of the large, four-poster feather bed. "Just pull this on if you get a bit of a chill tonight," Marie said.

"Thank you, Marie," Molly said. "I'm sure we'll be more than comfortable." The old, high-ceilinged bedroom seemed a bit old-fashioned, and there was a faint aroma of mothballs, but it was quite clean and welcoming, Molly thought. She sat down on the corner of the bed and pushed down on the feather mattress. It was soft but still firm. "Oh, is there anything more inviting than a comfortable bed at the end of a long day of traveling?" she said.

Susan sat down next to her and bounced gently. "Say, it is quite comfy. Ours seems to be as well," she said.

"I believe the beds are all in pretty much the same shape, as far as we noticed," Marie said. "We slept wonderfully last night. At any rate Molly, Victor and I will be right across the hall, and Susan and Richard will be in the room next to you. If you need anything, just knock on my door."

"Oh, that's fine," Molly said. "I'm sure I won't need to bother you. You two go on, now. No need to fuss over me. I'm just going to settle in and read a while before Sam comes up."

"Sounds good," Marie said. "Sleep well and we'll see you in the morning." Molly smiled and nodded and thanked Marie again.

Marie led Susan to her and Richard's room next to Molly and Sam's. Susan entered, and Marie turned to leave but Susan put her hand on Marie's arm.

"Are you sure you don't want to stay a while? Until the boys come up?" Susan asked. She forced a smile, but it didn't mask her unease.

"Now Susan, don't tell me you're still frightened from Martin reading that silly old journal?" Marie said.

Susan smiled with some embarrassment. "Just a little, I suppose."

Marie gave Susan a gentle hug. "So am I, I must admit," Marie said. "Come here." She got into the bed and pulled one of the blankets over her, and then she lifted up one edge of the covers invitingly.

Susan giggled and crawled in beside her. "Let's talk until the boys come up."

"Wait," Marie said, "One more thing." She got up and walked to the door, and fastened the deadbolt. "I feel better with that locked. I know it's silly of me...when the boys come up they can just knock for us to let them in." She hurried back to the bed and under the covers next to Susan.

***

Richard took another sip of brandy as he and Sam finished their nightcap in the study.

"That's the craziest story I've ever heard, in that journal," Sam said. "Richard, you know I have nothing but respect for this family we've married into, but I have to think that the old man was just a bit off his rocker, eh?"

Richard inhaled deeply and sighed. He flashed a hint of a smile. "I've seen some odd things since I've been here, Sam. Some damned odd things."

"Look, when you get out to an isolated place in the country like this, it plays tricks on you. It plays tricks on all of us," Sam said. "I'm used to the streetcars and crowds in the city, always something going on. This type of place...out in the middle of nowhere? Everything seems strange."

Richard raised his eyebrows. "As you said, I'm a military man, Sam. I've spent time in some God-forsaken holes that should have been a hell of a lot more unnerving than this place. But that's the thing, Sam. They weren't."

Sam smiled and shook his head. "I'm sure there's nothing going on here at all. That journal was a bit creepy, I'll admit—but so is reading Poe. Probably just the old man's idea to stir up some interest in the place, to raise the value when he was looking to sell."

"Well, perhaps, Sam. Perhaps," Richard said, in the same tone of voice he would use with one of his inexperienced junior officers back in his army days.

Sam drained his glass and put it on the mantle. He raised his arms above his head, stretching as he yawned. "I'm going to step out for a breath of evening air," he said to Richard. "I'll see you in the morning." Richard half-drunkenly raised his glass to Sam and nodded.

Sam stepped out through the study's heavy French doors into the chilly night and the quiet yard. He breathed deeply as he walked outside and smelled the clean scent of pine and cold. Despite his complaints to the contrary, he had to admit that the country air could be rather invigorating.

He walked a few paces towards the tree line, and turned back to look at the house. The lights from the study and the upstairs bedrooms were subtle, comforting beacons in the midst of the darkness all around. And it *was* dark. And very quiet. The heavy isolation, equally peaceful and lonely, struck Sam the same way it would any city person when spending an evening in the country, particularly an overcast one like this. The only sound was the steady breeze rustling the crisp leaves on the ground. Sam took out a silver case from his breast pocket, pulled out a cigarette, and lit it. He inhaled deeply and looked up again at the strange old house, and at the bedroom window on the left. A figure passed behind it, and he was quite sure it was Molly. For all his cheerful confidence and bluster, he thought Molly was perhaps the only thing in life he had really gotten right. She could see right through his boasting and shallow humor, to the small, insecure, conflicted man that was underneath. Sometimes, Sam liked to think, it was that small, insignificant man that Molly really loved. He took a lot of things lightly in his life; Molly wasn't one of them. The tip of his cigarette glowed brightly as he took a long draw.

Someone was behind him.

The impression was instantaneous, and more from instinct than from any of his senses. Sam was not jumpy by nature, and he turned around neither slowly nor quickly. At first he didn't see anything, but then he caught movement out of the corner of his eye. Some thirty yards to his right, just on the edge of the trees he saw a figure, but just for a moment. It ducked back into the shadows, although it seemed to have a faint glow about it. Sam looked back at the house and a slight tingle went down his back. If it had been someone from the house, he would have heard them and probably seen them come out and walk down to the woods. Given the tone of the evening, he didn't suspect that anyone was in the mood to play a joke on him. Maybe it was some neighbor or other local walking around? But who would be out at this hour, and why would they come out here?

"Hey, is there something I can do for you?" Sam said. He had planned on sounding firm and confident, but the words came out sounding timid and tinny, and at a volume that was barely above normal conversation.

He scanned the woods again, focusing on the spot he had last seen the figure, but he couldn't make anything out. The silence was heavy; even the wind had stopped blowing. The figure appeared again, to the left now, and no more than fifteen yards from him. It didn't seem possible that the person could have moved that far, that quickly. The figure was walking away from Sam, and now he could clearly make out that it was a woman. She was wearing a long dress, not white, but dull and light-colored. She seemed to have a hood or veil over her head. She moved quickly towards the other side of yard, and she was carrying a small lantern in her right hand. It wasn't glowing brightly, but it still shone clearly against the moonless curtain of the night's darkness.

"Hey! Hey, Miss!" Sam yelled out, but the figure continued moving rapidly away, back into the woods. Sam followed. He was now getting annoyed. He knew that he didn't completely understand the country way of life, but sneaking up at night on somebody's property had to be out of bounds. If she was a neighbor that was out for a walk, she could have stopped and said something. Weren't country people supposed to be friendly?

He walked quickly after her, and he just got a glimpse of the lantern from behind a big elm, one that was just on the outer edge of the yard. How did she get that far so quickly? A few yards past the elm were the patches of brambles and wild grape vines that enveloped the deeper woods.

So she was behind that tree. He'd put a good scare into her. He kept his eye on the elm to make sure she didn't come out on either side, and he half jogged up to the tree. He reached the elm and rested his left hand on the rough bark, leaning on the tree as he tried to catch his breath without making any excessive noise. *Too many cigarettes. He definitely should cut down.* After a few seconds, he readied himself and then quickly swung around the tree to confront the woman.

"Hey, I just want to..." Sam stopped in mid-sentence. The hooded figure turned to face him, and it was then that Sam realized that the figure he was pursuing wasn't human. At least not anymore. Its face was desiccated and half-gone, and was as crumbling as centuries-old parchment. Sam felt his breath simply stop as the figure looked him in the eye and slowly smiled. It was the teeth that Sam would later remember in his nightmares. Flawless, brilliantly white and perfectly proportioned teeth appeared like lustrous pearls beneath the corrupted, cracked, gray-brown lips that hardly seemed capable of smiling.

For all his terror and revulsion, Sam was still left with some subconscious appreciation that this creature had once been beautiful. The smile, however, was more cruel and malignant than Sam had ever seen on any living person. He stepped backwards and tried to turn, but his forearm was suddenly seized by the thing. The papery, dry hand of the creature grabbed him like a claw, and with a strength that surprised Sam. He tried to pull away, and he wasn't sure if the crackling and crunching he heard was the dry leaves beneath his feet or the straining of the creature's withered musculature.

For an instant he felt as if he might break free, but then his arm was snapped back and he was pulled up close the creature, their faces only inches apart. The thing was still smiling its hideous smile, and Sam felt his own lips quivering as the creature let out a slow, guttural hiss. Its breath was hot and dry, and carried the stench of ancient death from arid, desolate lands. Sam pulled away again, but to no avail. The grip of the thing was still vice-like. It pressed its mouth to his neck, and Sam felt a wince of pain. He heard himself let out a small sob, and then, just as his legs gave out beneath him he felt the creature's grip relax. Sam fell to the ground on his backside, and whimpered as he began to scoot backwards. He looked up for the creature and saw nothing; it had vanished, silently. He became aware that the wind had picked up slightly, and the crunching of the leaves beneath him was the only sound in the otherwise still evening.

Sam staggered to his feet, and half-ran, half-stumbled back the way he had come. Or at least it was the way he thought he had come. He didn't think he had gone that far from the house, but all he could see were trees on all sides, and after a few moments he was no longer sure which way the house even was. Nothing looked familiar, and there seemed to be many more tall evergreens than he remembered. He stopped and looked around. He thought he saw a faint light rising above the trees in the distance. Sam wasn't completely sure that the light was coming from the house, but he didn't have any better ideas. He began staggering in that general direction.

Chapter Five

The fire was settled and comfortable, with a gentle flame licking a piece of split elm in the grate above a nice bed of glowing embers. Victor was sitting in a nearby upholstered chair, reading further in his grandfather's journal. Martin, a glass of wine in his hand, strolled over to the bureau in the corner. There were several thick books on top, and Martin flipped through them, noting the titles.

"What are these, Victor? *Relics of Ra. Tutankhamen Era Egyptian Art. Religious Totems of Ancient Egypt.*"

"What? Oh yes, Jameson told me about them," Victor said. "They just arrived the other day, he said. Some of the last books that Grandfather ordered, apparently. I didn't look them over too closely."

"Well, let's see what we can find," Martin said, as he scanned the table of contents of Relics of Ra. "I'm somewhat familiar with the lineages and dynasties, but I'm a little weak on the actual relics and artifacts."

The two men read in silence for a few minutes, when Martin interjected excitedly. "Victor, take a look at this." Victor put his own book down, got up and walked over to Martin.

"What have you got?" Victor asked.

"This statue here," Martin said, pointing to a photograph in the book. He turned to Victor. "It's just like the one in the foyer."

Victor looked closely at the illustration Martin was pointing to. "The one with the strange crown, holding the staff? Yes...I think you're right," he said, reading the description in the book. "Statue of Sekhmet, Eleventh Dynasty..."

***

Richard was slumped in his chair in the study. He was both tired and drunk, and he struggled to keep his eyes open. His body was losing the battle to maintain consciousness, but as his chin tilted forward onto his chest, he became dimly aware of a rattling sound. His mind first placed the noise in the hazy context of the start of some vague dream, but then he fully awoke. The sound was not a dream. It was the handle of the door to the study. Richard hadn't noticed at the time, but he assumed that Sam must have closed the door when he left. Now he must be trying to get back in, Richard thought, and he couldn't seem to get the latch.

"Just pull the damned door open, Sam, for Christ's sake," Richard said, still groggy.

Richard's eyes were still unfocused when the door exploded open with a force that was well beyond the strength of Sam, or any human. A spray of wood splinters hit him in the face and chest, and the top hinge broke as the door smashed back against the wall. Despite the alcohol and exhaustion, Richard's military training kicked in and reflexively he was on his feet and facing the intruder.

It was a woman, Richard concluded, or at least it had been at some distant point in time. It was wearing a dull white robe, and its head and face were covered with a faded, half-threadbare veil. It stood silhouetted in the archway, as the shattered door swung and creaked weakly on its one remaining hinge. Richard thought he could just make out a horrible grin of white teeth showing past the yellowed, desiccated mouth of the thing under the veil, but he wasn't sure. What registered most clearly to him was the long blade in the thing's right hand. It wasn't quite sword-length, but it was a good deal longer than an ordinary knife. The blade had a slight scimitar curve, but despite Richard's wide knowledge of modern bladed weapons from various cultures, he didn't recognize the design. The thing hissed slowly at Richard as it took a step forward, but if it thought Richard would be paralyzed with fear, it was mistaken.

Richard took a step towards the thing, and then lunged to his left. He stepped one foot on the upholstered chair and reached up to the wall, where old Warren Adams had mounted a pair of antique sabers for display. Richard grabbed one of the sabers, and as he stepped back into a classic defensive stance he briefly marveled at the balance and heft of the weapon—it was a *real* saber, not one made for decoration. He had little time for reflection, however, as the thing in white came in fast, slashing down with its weapon at Richard's head. The thing's speed seemed uncanny, and Richard's fencing days were several years in the past. Despite these facts, and even with the copious amount of alcohol in his system, Richard clearly read the thing's incoming attack. Still, he was a fraction of second slow. As he used his own blade to parry the downward slash to his left, the tip of the thing's blade caught his shoulder, drawing blood. Richard riposted instantly, as his training had taught him. He cut across to the right with his palm down. The thing lurched backwards with incredible speed. Richard wasn't clear if his cut had been a bit short of his target, or if his opponent was actually insubstantial, but any rate his slash did not connect with the thing.

"Come on now," Richard said, slightly slurring his words. "We're just getting started."

The thing hissed again behind its veil, and began to growl. The sound was weird and unsettling, and Richard thought that it sounded more feline than human. He didn't see the profit in sitting back and waiting for the thing's next move, so he went on the attack, putting all his weight and focus into one of the most perfect thrusts that he had ever delivered ("Hand before foot," he remembered his old fencing master always admonishing him.) With inhuman reflexes the thing twisted out of the way, and then dropped its own blade, stepped forward and closed the gap. It grasped Richard's sword-hand with its left hand, and Richard's throat with its right, and subconsciously Richard marveled at the strength of the thing's papery, bone-dry fingers. He could smell the fetid desert breath of the creature, its veiled face just inches from his own, and he felt his own strength fading. He flashed the thing a wry smile. There would be no pleas for mercy. Richard was deeply aware of his own human flaws, but he lived as a man, and he would die as one. Richard's grip weakened, and his saber fell to the floor. He could feel his consciousness fading, and he became sickly aware that the thing was lapping at the wound on his shoulder like a cat at a bowl of milk...and then, it was sucking.

"Richard, what's going on?" Victor yelled, as he and Martin came running from the other room. The thing snarled and turned its head towards the voices. The lower half of its veil was wet and red with blood. It gave one last, contemptuous look at Richard, and as Victor and Martin burst into the study, the thing threw Richard to the floor. Victor came in first, stopped and stepped back in horror at the scene he was witnessing. Martin ran straight into Victor's back, unsure of what was happening. Before he could get his bearings, something in white rushed by him. The thing's speed was unnatural, and Martin couldn't make out what it was. Victor looked to where the creature had gone, but he couldn't see anything. He rushed over to Richard.

"Are you all right?" Victor said. He noticed the blood running down Richard's shoulder and arm. "What happened? What was that?"

"What's going on?" Martin said, completely confused.

Richard got to his knees, and he rubbed his throat, gasping for breath. He coughed, and then looked up at Victor and Martin. "Quite a...quite a timely entrance, I should say," he whispered, trying to get his voice back. "Greatly appreciated."

"What was it, Richard?" Victor asked again.

"Can't say that I rightly know," Richard said. "Never faced a foe quite like that."

"Was it…was it…*human*?" Victor asked.

"Don't think so, old man," Richard said, rising to his feet.

"What are you going on about?" Martin said. "Here," he took a white handkerchief out of his breast pocket and pressed it to Richard's wound. "You'll need to get your shirt off and have this properly tended," he said.

"Sam," Victor said. "Where is Sam?"

"I don't know," Richard said. I think he stepped out for some air."

***

Despite—or perhaps because of—the excitement of the evening, Susan and Marie were not long able to resist the call of sleep. Marie's eyelids became heavy, and as her arms gently relaxed her open volume of Shelley's poetry slowly came to rest just under her chin. The lamp was still on, and next to her Susan already breathed slowly and heavily in a deep, dreamless sleep. The room was still and quiet and neither of them saw the knob of the bedroom's door slowly begin to turn. There was pressure against the door and the knob rotated more forcefully, but the latched deadbolt prevented the door from opening. The knob began turning with more intensity, and the rattling got louder. Marie opened her eyes, unsure of where the sound was coming from. She leaned up on one elbow, and Susan also awoke. The doorknob continued turning quickly and rattling aggressively, followed by a forceful pushing of the door against the deadbolt.

"Who is it?" Susan hoarsely whispered to Marie. Marie looked back at Susan and shook her head.

"Who's there?" Marie shouted.

The doorknob continued to turn violently, and was now followed by a steady pounding on the door.

"Who's there?" Susan shouted, and she could hear the shaking in her own voice.

"It's me," came a half-whisper from the other side of the door. "It's Molly! Do let me in!" she said, as she continued to rattle and push at the door.

"Molly," Marie said, as she jumped out of bed and ran to unbolt the door. Molly quickly pushed her way into the room, and just as quickly turned and shut the door, pushing the deadbolt back into place.

"Oh, dear God," Molly said. "I saw something. I *saw* something!"

"What, Moll?' Susan asked. "What did you see?"

"It was horrible!" Molly said. "A woman...a face...oh, God. I don't know *what* it was. A ghost, maybe. Something. It's out there! Don't open the door!"

"Don't be silly, Moll," Marie said. "You've had a bad dream, that's all. You're all right. You're safe now. Come, I'll show you." Marie unbolted the door, and reached for the handle.

"No, please Marie, don't open it," Molly said, pleading. "I didn't dream anything. I hadn't even gone to sleep!"

"Look, there's nothing out there. I'll show you," Marie said as she turned the latch and started to open the door. Before she even realized what was happening, she felt a violent push, and the door jammed open against her shoulder. It was only ajar a couple inches, but she saw the dried, leathery hands that were trying to force it open further. Molly screamed, and Susan gasped and stepped backwards. Marie instinctively put her shoulder up against the door, and pushed as hard as she could to get it shut again. One dried hand wrapped its fingers around the door, and the other grasped the frame as the thing tried to pry the door open. Marie struggled, but could tell that whatever was on the other side of the door was far stronger than she was. Seeing what was happening, Molly darted to help Marie, and pushed at the door with both hands. A second later, Susan rushed forward and joined them.

Marie winced as she pushed at the door with all her might. She heard the thing hiss on the other side. The three of them together were winning the battle, and after a few more moments of struggle, it was over. All pressure from the thing ceased, and the door slammed shut. Marie latched the bolt as fast as she could.

"I was watching its hands," Susan said. "It didn't pull them back. They just... vanished. Disappeared."

"That's what I saw, as well," Molly said.

"I had my head turned the other way. I couldn't see it," Marie said.

Susan let out a small scream as they heard the sound of footsteps and commotion in the hallway. Whatever it was was getting closer, and coming towards their room. The three stepped back as they heard the first heavy strike against the door, followed by a violent pounding and rattling of the doorknob again.

"Marie! Susan! Are you all right?"

It was Victor! Molly sighed in relief.

"Thank God," Susan said.

Marie undid the bolt and opened the door, and Victor, Martin and Richard scrambled in. Richard closed and bolted the door behind him.

Marie rushed to Victor and hugged him tightly. "It was trying to get in, Victor. It's real. I could see its hands..."

"We know, dear. We've seen it too," Victor said. He kissed his wife on the forehead and brought his cheek to hers, his eyes closed in relief.

"Sam!" Molly said. "Where is Sam?"

Richard took Molly by the shoulders and looked her in the eyes. "He's not with us. He wasn't downstairs. He said he was going out for a walk earlier, and that's the last we've seen of him."

"Well, we have to go find him," Molly said, looking back and forth at the others.

"We *will,* Molly," Richard said. "But we have to deal with first things first."

"Richard dear, you're hurt," Susan said, noticing the wound on her husband's shoulder.

Richard shook his head and turned to Marie, and then back to Molly. "What's been going on up here?" he said.

"What did you see, Molly? Was it in your room?" Marie asked.

"It was horrible," Molly said. "I wasn't asleep yet. I had just put out the lamp next to me by the bed, but I left the other one on for... for when Sam came up. I suddenly got the strangest feeling, as if someone else was in the room. Of course I knew no one else had come in, but I couldn't shake the sensation. I looked around...the light was so dim. I saw something in the corner, a figure, maybe. I stared at it, but nothing moved. I was sure it was just a coat or a nightshirt hanging on the wall." Molly sobbed, and Marie put her arm around her.

"Go on, Moll," Marie said.

Molly nodded weakly. "I...I knew I couldn't get to sleep until I was sure. You know how your mind plays tricks on you? So I told myself to be brave, and just get up and make sure that it was a coat or blouse hanging on the wall. I walked over to it quickly, and still nothing moved. As I got almost to it, I could see it was a figure. Completely still. As my eyes started to focus, it...*looked up at me*. Oh God, that awful smile!" Molly burst into tears, and Marie hugged her and patted her back.

"And then she came running to our room," Susan said. "And then that thing tried to get in here, but we kept it out."

"What are we going to do?" Marie said to her husband.

"Martin," Victor said. "That book you were reading from."

"*Relics of Ra*", Martin said, holding it up. "I still have it with me."

Victor turned to the others. "From what Martin was reading, Grandfather was probably right. This...thing, whatever it is, is somehow related to that statue of Sekhmet."

"But how does that help us?" Susan said.

Victor looked over at Martin. "What does the book say?"

"Erm...yes," Martin said, adjusting his glasses. He found the page in the book, and began reading. *"According to Egyptian legend, Hathor was the bride of Ra, the king of the gods. She personified joy, feminine love, and motherhood. When Ra discovered that the humans were plotting against him, he transformed Hathor into Sekhmet, a bloodthirsty warrior princess, and sent her to wreak vengeance on the humans."*

"Sekhmet?" Richard said.

"But how did she get here?" Molly asked.

"Who knows?" Victor said. "Grandfather was the expert on these matters. He could read and speak ancient Egyptian. He has boxes and boxes of notes and translations packed away here. Maybe he read some incantation, and it called out something from the statue?"

"Some curse for robbing the tombs?" Susan asked. "I'm sure I read something about that. The Carter expedition, wasn't it? Didn't many of them die in mysterious circumstances?"

"Rubbish," said Martin. "Those men died of normal causes—just a few coincidences in there that were made a great deal of by the popular press. And besides, Grandfather wasn't involved in any of those excavations."

"If you have a better explanation for our situation, brother, I'm all ears," Victor said.

Martin rubbed his chin. He didn't have a response.

"Does that really matter at this point?" Richard asked. "Let's deal with facts. We know it's here. Can we fight it? I think that's the pertinent question at this point. I didn't have much luck with a saber, and with all due modesty, I doubt any of you could fare better."

"Does the book give any advice, Martin?" Victor asked.

Martin ran his index figure down the page. "*...after Sekhmet was sent down to the world of men, her slaughter and bloodlust became uncontrollable—she was on the verge of destroying all of humanity. Ra deceived her by pouring out beer dyed red with ochre. Mistaking it for blood, Sekhmet drank, and becoming intoxicated, she...transformed back into the benevolent Hathor.*"

"I'm not sure where we're going to get any red beer," Susan said.

“Wine!” Victor said. "There are a half-dozen bottles in the kitchen."

Richard raised his eyebrows, and Marie nodded enthusiastically.

“Yes, but you aren’t taking this book seriously, are you?" Martin asked. "It’s mostly just scholarly speculation, from a few translated texts of mythology. Historians and archeologists really know comparatively little about how seriously even the ancient Egyptians took these tales.”

“I’d say it’s worth a try,” Richard said. “That thing out there isn’t ‘scholarly speculation’.”

“It certainly isn’t,” Molly said. “And we need to get down there and find Sam. He may be in trouble.”

“How are we going to get downstairs with it right out there?” Susan asked.

“Wait, there’s more here,” Martin said, scanning the book intently. “It says the creature was supposedly repelled by any holy object. Sekhmet was forbidden from destroying anyone still loyal to Ra.”

“I hate to mention this, Martin,” Marie said, “but I really don’t think we have any ancient Egyptian holy objects lying about. And I don’t think any of us here are still loyal to Ra.”

Martin adjusted his glasses and looked up at Marie. “Well it doesn’t say ‘Egyptian’ holy objects, specifically. Who has a cross?”

“I suppose I have one,” Susan said, pulling a small silver cross out from the chain around her neck.

“I do too,” Marie said. “Do you have one, Molly?

“No, but I have this,” She said, reaching to her neck to retrieve a small locket. She opened it. “It’s St. Peter.”

“Excellent,” Victor said. He spotted something on the bureau, and reached for it. “And here’s a Bible.”

“I don't know,” Susan said. “Crosses? Bibles? Isn't this a bit preposterous?”

“The whole thing is preposterous, dear, but here we are,” Richard said. He turned to the others. “I’ll stick with this,” he said, holding up his saber. Turning the handle, he looked intently at both sides of the blade. “I’ll be ready for it this time.”

Victor held his Bible in hand as he slowly opened the door. Richard braced himself, his saber at the ready. The door creaked, and Victor flung the door open. Susan gasped, but there was nothing there. The hallway was empty and silent.

Victor cast a glance at his wife, and Marie met his gaze. She smiled and nodded confidently.

“Let’s go,” Victor said, and stepped out into the hallway. Richard held the door as each of them went through, all moving silently. Richard came last, walking backwards with his saber at the ready as he guarded the rear flank. The group made their way to the stairs and down to the living room.

“Well, that wasn’t too bad,” Martin said, “all things considered.”

Richard walked over to a small ivory statue sitting on a shelf on the wall. “Is this it?” he asked.

Martin walked over and picked up the statue. “Yes. Grandfather had it in the foyer, and we just brought it in here,” he said. He looked down at the book and turned several pages. “Yes, this is it," he said, pointing at an illustration.

"Well then," Richard said, taking the statue and examining it, "why don't you—"

The big French doors looking over the back yard burst open, the force breaking the panes and sending shards of glass all over the living room. Susan screamed, and Richard stepped back as the thing in white flew through the maelstrom of debris into the room. It landed, bracing itself with one leathery hand against the bookcase. It hissed in rage and scanned the room slowly, staring at each of the humans in turn. It again flashed its hellish smile from underneath its faded, blood-stained veil.

Richard held up the statue in his left hand and smiled back at the thing. He lifted his saber with his right hand, but the creature was on him in an instant. It hit Richard with incredible force, and slammed him against the back wall. The thing then turned towards Victor, and advanced.

"Quick, block the exits!" Victor yelled, holding up his Bible against the thing. The others moved into position.

The creature stepped back with a guttural, feline growl and turned back to the dazed, staggering Richard to finish him off.

"Victor!" Richard yelled, and he tossed the statue. Victor caught it, and took a step forward towards the creature, brandishing the statue in one hand, and his Bible in the other. The thing hesitated, snarling. Victor stood his ground, and then saw something green fly past his head towards the creature.

"There, try that!" Martin yelled. The half full bottle of Bordeaux smashed on the hardwood floor at the creature's feet. It growled at Victor and took another step forward, but then looked down at the spreading pool of dark-red wine. It hesitated, then crouched down and slowly put one leathery finger down into the liquid, and brought it back to its lips. It paused for a moment, and then bent all the way down and began lapping at the puddle.

"*It's drinking!*" Martin half-whispered.

"Marie, get a couple more bottles from the kitchen!" Victor shouted. Marie nodded and hurried off. She returned a moment later with two bottles under her arm and one in her hand. Victor dropped the statue and took one of the bottles from her.

Susan held her cross out towards the creature, and Molly did the same with her locket, but the creature didn't seem to be paying them any attention. It was still lapping at the wine on the floor.

"Stand back," Victor said. He took a full bottle of wine and smashed its top off on the corner of the table. He then walked over to the creature and poured that bottle onto the floor as well. The thing snarled slightly, but otherwise ignored Victor as it lapped and slurped at the wine with a focused intensity. Richard broke the top off another bottle and poured out more for the thing. As the creature continued drinking, its low growling was beginning to change in tone. It was sounding less like the aggressive snarl of a feral beast and more like the plaintive moans of a much different creature, one recognizably human.

"Its hands—look at its hands," Marie said. The creature's hands were no longer wrinkled and shriveled, but were transforming into the delicate hands of a young woman.

"What in blazes?" Richard asked, as he lowered his saber.

"Wine, in place of blood..." Martin said.

The creature stood up slowly, and wobbled a bit. It walked

towards Victor, who took a step backwards in response. It then turned to Marie, who also retreated. It scanned the horrified faces of all in the room. The creature took a step backwards, still unsteady on its feet. It then brought both hands up, and slowly pulled the veil from its face. Gone was the desiccated, parchment-like skin and in its place was the smooth, radiant, dark-eyed visage of a beautiful woman, her jet-black hair shining and shimmering. It smiled, and instead of the cruel, hellish grin it had displayed before, it now conveyed only a gentle benevolence and a vulnerable kindness.

The creature that was now Hathor looked around the room and made eye contact with each of them, and its expression conveyed a mixture of regret, confusion and warm sympathy. It fixed its gaze on Molly, and stepped towards her. Molly stood transfixed, unable to move. The thing stood before her, and then it slowly reached its hand out to Molly's belly, and touched it gently. It looked Molly in the eyes again and smiled, and Molly nodded and smiled back. The creature turned and began walking towards the open, smashed window, but after only a few steps it began to shimmer, and then in silence it vanished completely.

"Martin," Victor said calmly, "Why don't you destroy the statue."

Martin picked the statue of Sekhmet off the floor where it had fallen, looked at it a moment, and then with all his might threw it against the fieldstone fireplace, where it smashed to bits. The group stood in silence for a moment, as a strange scent of ancient, unknown spice and perfume slowly permeated the room. Susan rushed over to Richard, who, with some effort, got to his feet.

The door to the back walkway began rattling, and Victor turned sharply. Marie ran to him, and he put his arm around her protectively. She gasped as the door slowly opened.

“You wouldn’t believe what happened to me out there,” Sam said, as he came through the door. Molly cried out and ran to him, and furiously kissed him.

“What’s all this about?” Sam said.

“What happened to you?” Susan asked.

“I…I don’t know. I went out for a walk, and saw someone…I don’t remember much of anything else.” He rubbed his neck and winced. He pulled his hand back and noticed dried blood on his fingers. “Seems like I got some kind of scratch, or bite, out there…” Molly took Sam’s handkerchief out of his shirt pocket and pressed it to the small wound on his neck.

Martin shook his head, and looked over at Victor. “If I hadn’t seen all this, I’d have never believed it.”

“Why did it approach you like that, Molly?” Marie asked.

“I…I hadn’t told anyone yet—not even Sam. The fact of the matter is…I’m pregnant. How it knew, I haven’t the foggiest idea. It was…happy for me. Genuinely happy. I could feel that.”

“Pregnant? We’re going to have a baby?” Sam asked, rushing over to Molly.

“That’s wonderful!” Marie said, and Susan also hurried over to give Molly a hug.

Richard smiled, and then walked over to Victor and put his hand on his shoulder. “What do you make of all this, old man?”

“I’m not sure we’ll ever know,” Victor said. He bent down and picked up a piece of the shattered statue and examined it. “Maybe now," he said, as he tossed the shard into the fireplace and looked out the smashed window, "she can finally rest in peace."

Europa Solitaire

"Read them and weep, Albert," Commander Evgeny Karlamov said. "Aces and jacks."

He put his cards down face-up, and reached for the pot of Cadbury chocolate bars, tiny bottles of bourbon and vodka, and a cellophane-wrapped cigar. "This will clean you out, I think." Evgeny had quite a pile of winnings in front of him.

Captain Albert Freese, in contrast, was down to a small bag of Russian hard candy and a gold-colored ring that didn't look very old or valuable.

Still looking at his cards, Freese put his hand on top of Evgeny's and the pot. "Hold on, my friend," he said. "I have these." He smiled as he looked Evgeny in the eye and spread his cards on the table. "Three nines."

"I thought you said you never played poker before this mission?" Evgeny said, frowning and pulling his hand back, leaving the pot to his captain.

"The game is luck, not skill," Freese said, grinning. "Like most card games. That's why you win so much. I've never been lucky. And that's why you won't play chess, a game of skill and intelligence."

"There is skill involved in poker," Evgeny said. He sat back in his chair and folded his arms behind his head. "But yes, luck is big part of it. You get dealt your hand, and you play it as best you can. That is life, my friend. You don't know what's coming, and you can't plan everything five moves ahead, like chess. But I told you, we'll play chess on the way back. I do have some experience with that game. I am Russian, after all." Evgeny bit off the end of the cigar and lit it. He took a big puff, and then handed it over to Freese, who also took a long draw. He raised his eyebrows in appreciation and handed it back to Evgeny.

The calm, matronly voice of the ship's computer came over the intercom. "Tolstoy-1 entering Jupiter approach phase, time 22:41 UGE, within tolerance of schedule. Orbit insertion maneuver will commence in seven hours, sixteen minutes. First contact range with Europa in eighteen hours, ten minutes."

"All right, sounds like we're on track. Let's get to work," Freese said.

The control room was small and the walls and fixtures were white, but the lighting was warm and calming. The two men stood over a large table displaying a colorful holographic image of the moon Europa.

"Let's go over this one more time," Freese said. "At 17:12 UGE tomorrow, we do our first fly-by of Europa. You're going to pilot the jump shuttle, and after launch you should get through the atmosphere and down to the ice in just under three hours. We should be able to set you down within ten meters of the Pellucidar-7A. From everything it's been feeding back to us, it had a fairly soft landing when it came down three years ago, and the only thing that conked out was a circuit on the solar converter. You replace that, flip it on, and shoot back up here, and we continue the rest of the survey mission. We've run through it a hundred times, so I know you don't have any questions. But do you have any questions?"

Evgeny shook his head and smiled. "I know drill," he said.

"Just remember to wear your wool gloves and a hat," Freese said. "It gets cold down there."

"Maybe cold for you from California," Commander Evgeny Karlamov said. "I grew up in cold. I will be right at home."

"Seriously, Evgeny, pay attention to your temperature display. Constantly. Don't ignore the audio warnings. These suits are fantastic, but it's -120 down there on a hot day. You know you won't have much time to get back to the shuttle if you have problems. You'll freeze up like a Russian popsicle in about half a second," Freese said.

***

They spent another two hours going over the details and checking the latest telemetry readings of the conditions on Europa. The mission was simple. Four years ago the Pellucidar-7A probe had been launched with the sole purpose of touching down on Jupiter's moon Europa. All indications were that Europa had vast saltwater oceans in liquid form—oceans comparable in volume to all the seas on Earth. Further indications were that undersea volcanoes on Europa, combined with tidal interactions with Jupiter, might very well heat the ocean enough to provide a suitable environment for some kind of life. The problem was that the surface temperature of Europa was so cold that the entire moon was covered with a thick sheet of ice. That's where the Pellucidar-7A probe was supposed to shine. It was a melting probe, and was designed to land on an area where the ice sheet was at its thinnest—perhaps no more than six or eight kilometers. With a flash heating system it would melt its way down through the ice to the liquid ocean, and then assume its primary function as an undersea probe, transmitting data back to Earth.

Everything had gone well with the probe's launch, and it had landed almost precisely where it was supposed to—no small feat of engineering. The melting phase of the mission was a no-go, however. The heating device simply failed to engage. NASA and the Russian Space Agency had spent over $4 billion on this mission, and it was the first launched under the auspices of the fledgling Union of Greater Earth. They weren't keen on abandoning it as a failure. With the successful development and recent deployment of the Japanese-designed one-man jump shuttle, it had become feasible to send astronauts down to a planet's surface from an orbiting ship, and so the repair of the Pellucidar-7A was added to the flight itinerary of the Tolstoy-1 and its two-man crew consisting of Captain Albert Freese and Commander Evgeny Karlamov.

Evgeny was making the final adjustments in the jump shuttle prior to its launch. He was fully enveloped in his metallic gray enviro-suit, all except for the helmet, and he again marveled at how incredibly light and comfortable the suit was. The space suits that Evgeny had first trained in at the academy, just ten years ago, were three times as heavy and offered half the mobility. He lowered himself in from the top, and fit comfortably into the man-shaped indentation that was the cockpit.

The ship's computer sounded again. "Launch of jump shuttle in ten minutes, thirty seconds."

"How is it looking, Evgeny?" Captain Freese said from the control room. "Everything checks out up here. Can you switch on your external view screen?"

"Check, Captain," Evgeny said. He flicked the switch for the screen, and the wide panel in front of him came brilliantly to life with the blue-orange image of Europa appearing, magnificent in front of its endless black starfield backdrop.

"That looks good up here," Freese said. "I haven't seen any geysers from the surface yet, but keep an eye out for them. You don't need to be going through one of those if you can help it." Geysers on Europa regularly shot plumes of salt-water mist hundreds of kilometers into the atmosphere.

"Understood, Captain," Evgeny said. He made one final check of the system indicators. Perfect. "All systems active and normal. Ready for launch, captain."

With just under five minutes to launch, Freese did a last scan of Europa's surface when something caught his eye. "Hold it, Evgeny. I'm seeing a geyser forming. Southern hemisphere, about 1500 kilometers south-southwest of your landing site."

"Yes, I see it," Evgeny said. "Not a problem. Not in flight path."

"Roger that," Freese said. "Launch in 30 seconds." He held his breath. It didn't matter how normal all the readings and telemetry were, if things were going to go badly, this is often when they did. "...three, two, one...and...launch."

The jump shuttle shot perfectly out of its bay, and Freese exhaled in relief and muttered a short prayer of thanks as the craft settled into its planned trajectory out and down to Europa. Evgeny was on his stomach flying head-first in the small one-man jump shuttle, and although they had both practiced this launch numerous times in simulated flights, none compared to the real thing.

Freese watched the tiny speck that was his colleague and friend as it steadily sailed through the endless, ink-black space and into the atmosphere of the moon. The red-orange cracks across the surface of Europa contrasted sharply with the ice-white surface and blue poles, and Freese soon lost sight of the tiny shuttle.

Two hours later, things were still progressing positively.

"How are we doing, Evgeny?"

"Everything reads normal, Captain," Evgeny said. The audio was clear. "Preparing for touchdown in twenty five...twenty four minutes."

"Geyser to your left, take a look at that," Freese said. The gray-white plume of salt water was easily a kilometer in diameter, and already dozens high as it slowly rose upward into space, gradually dissolving.

"Magnificent, Captain," Evgeny said.

"And are you reading normal? You, the human being, I mean," Freese said.

"Different than simulation, Captain. Very different."

"Just remember all the steps, Evgeny. You don't have to reinvent the wheel," Freese said.

The jump shuttle followed the flight plan nearly perfectly, and set down within several meters of the target. Despite the fact that this landing had been precisely planned and engineered by a veritable army of brilliant men, Freese was a pessimist by nature, and he felt no little degree of surprise that things were actually going as intended.

"Have touched down on Europa, Captain," Evgeny radioed.

"According to data, I am no more than 235 meters...south-south-west...from Pellucidar-7A. Am preparing for exit from shuttle."

"Great, Evgeny. Now don't forget to put your helmet on before you step outside," Freese said.

"Thanks for reminder," Evgeny said. "What would I do without you? In airlock....pressure adjusting...exiting shuttle...now."

Evgeny's video and audio feeds were coming through the main view screen on the Tolstoy-1, and Freese stared at the screen with rapt attention.

"Are you seeing this, Captain?" Evgeny asked.

"Signal coming through clear," Freese said. There was no atmosphere on Europa, and of course that meant no sky color, no wind, no weather. Freese wasn't expecting any dazzling views, but he was taken aback by the images on the screen. The icy, flat landscape stretching out to the horizon contrasted sharply with the black of space that enveloped all. He had seen the footage of previous probes, and the simulations, but this was something different. He took a long puff on his cigar, and shook his head, smiling.

"Measured strides out there, Evgeny—you're not Superman," Freese said. With Europa's gravity at less than one-fifth that of Earth's, it was common for astronauts in the simulators to take exaggerated leaps and strides, as they reveled in their new physical capabilities. That didn't always make for the most efficient use of the limited energy of the enviro-suit, however, and a system of regulated striding had been developed for low-gravity environments.

Evgeny continued ahead on the icy surface, and the only sound accompanying his video feed was his breathing.

"You should be within 100 meters now, Evgeny. You're right in line with the probe—part of it should still be above the surface. Do you see it?"

"Nyet," Evgeny said. "Not yet. Hold....yes. To my left...ahead. Do you see it, Captain?"

Freese pointed at the big screen as he walked a step closer to it. He could just make out a dark, oddly shaped mound, partially covered in snow and ice, some meters up ahead. "I've got it, Evgeny. That has to be it. Let's get that converter switched out, and get back to your shuttle."

"Don't worry, Captain. We are in good shape," Evgeny said.

Freese checked the telemetry readouts from Evgeny's suit. Temperature, oxygen, pressure—all normal. "Then let's get in and out while that's still the case."

Freese had just turned away from the screen for a second, and if there had been anything to see, he missed it. Evgeny's half-swallowed scream came through clearly enough, however, and when Freese turned back to the monitor all he could see was chaos. Evgeny was clearly stumbling, or falling, or both. For a moment Freese saw only the great black starfield above the moon, and then the video feed went blank.

"Evgeny! Come in! Evgeny! Are you all right?!" Silence. Freese frantically checked the vital readouts from Evgeny's suit. He was alive, and his suit was not damaged. "Evgeny! Respond!" Nothing.

***

Freese stared at the blank video monitor. It had been half an hour since he'd lost contact with Evgeny. He could see that Evgeny's vital readings were unchanged; he was still alive. His pulse was slow, in that gray area between awake and sleep. Had he been knocked out? Or was it only his communications that were damaged in the fall? Freese ran his palm down his face and over his beard. Evgeny had a good six hours of oxygen, so that wasn't an immediate concern. If he made it back to the jump shuttle, he could use the comlink there to resume contact with the Tolstoy 1. All he could do for the moment was wait, Freese thought.

He didn't have to wait long. A voice crackled over the audio feed. "Captain...I am...there is..." It was Evgeny, but it wasn't only Evgeny. Freese could swear that he heard another voice in the background. Indistinct, muffled, but not Evgeny, he was sure of that.

"What's going on, Evgeny? Are you all right?" Freese asked, trying to conceal his emotions.

"I am all right, Captain. He...is here with me...," Evgeny said. His voice was strong, but halting. "He has told me to deactivate video feed."

"What do you mean, 'he'? What are you talking about? *Who*?" Freese said. He was certain that Evgeny was injured, and was now delusional.

"He is not a...man, Captain. But he is here. We didn't know. We didn't know."

Freese couldn't tell if those last words were said to him, or to someone...*something* ...else.

"Commander Karlamov, make your way back to the jump shuttle immediately. *That's an order, Commander. Move, now!*" Freese said.

"I cannot do that Captain. He...says he...has things to show me. Things...that I must see."

"Who is telling you this, Evgeny? There's nobody here on this whole moon other than you and me. Are you physically able to get back to the shuttle?" Freese asked.

"He is not a man, Captain. They are not men. He does not speak, but he tells me. I must go with him," Evgeny said.

"Go where, Evgeny? With *who*?"

"Under the ice, Captain. To the oceans. Where the probe was to go. I will go, instead. There is much to see there, I am told," Evgeny said.

"You aren't equipped for anything like that, Evgeny. Go back to the shuttle, or you'll die there."

"I don't think I die, Captain. Not yet," Evgeny said. "But I must know. I must find out...why. I am...curious...for many things..."

"Evgeny, you're not well. You took a fall, and you're having trouble focusing. Remember the mission. You were just going to change the converter..."

"...the solar converter in the Pellucidar-7A," Evgeny said. "I am uninjured. My head is clear, Captain. But I must go with him," Evgeny said. "I must know."

"Look, if you don't get back to the jump shuttle within five hours, the Tolstoy-1 will be out of range...you wouldn't be able to launch again for another....

"For another two months, six days and thirty-five minutes, Captain," Evgeny said. "I have been told that I will be back to the shuttle at that time. You have sufficient supplies and power to wait that long for me. Please, Captain. Wait for me," Evgeny said.

"I don't understand," Freese said. "*Who* are you going with?"

"Back home I go to church, Captain. Orthodox," he said. His voice was stronger now. "There is old Russian hymn, by Dmitri Bortniansky, of St. Petersburg. It is called 'Come, O Thou Traveler Unknown.'" Do you know it?" Evgeny asked.

"No, I don't," Freese said. "Evgeny, you need to listen—"

"The story is from Genesis, Captain. When Jacob wrestled the angel. He had to know the angel's name. I must know. Please, for our friendship, Captain—wait for me."

***

Freese knew that he'd have to come up with some story to tell UGE Command as to why he was going to have to extend the mission another two months. Maybe he'd tell the truth, maybe something else. It didn't really matter. And anyways, what could they do from Earth? The Tolstoy-1 was well-equipped for a mission extension of this length, and he was the Captain.

After dinner that evening, Freese brought up the computer chess program on the main view screen. He had more than two months to kill, and he figured he could improve his game considerably in that time. He looked at the screen for a moment, and the vivid 3-D chessboard waited for his first move. He paused, and then shut off the screen. He pulled out the worn deck of cards that he and Evgeny played poker with. Evgeny often played solitaire, and he had shown Freese how to play. Maybe he'd give that a try, Freese thought. After all, he did have the time.

The Yokai of Lake Shinji

"So what are we supposed to do, just walk right up to Boss Endo and ask him for a job?" Ikko asked. He hurried to keep up with his taller partner, who strode confidently over the dirt streets of the bustling town.

"Something like that," Hiroji said. He hadn't shaved in several days, and his worn black *hakama* had gone without washing for much longer than that, but he still carried himself with the calm power of the samurai he was. Or once was, at least. "I've been hearing some things. I've got some ideas. What's your experience with *yokai*, Ikko?"

"Y*okai*? Demons...monsters? I know enough that I don't want to meet up with any," Ikko said. "Oh sure, it's all around town. Something's been seen up by Lake Shinji—is that what you're talking about?" They passed a pretty woman in a white and orange kimono selling rice balls from a cart, and she caught Ikko's eye and smiled. Ikko turned as he kept going and walked backwards a few steps, his eyes more focused on the glorious rice balls than the woman. He hadn't eaten since yesterday morning, when he and Hiroji first arrived in town. He rubbed the stubble on his chin and turned back around to catch up to Hiroji.

"That's exactly what I'm talking about," Hiroji said. "Rumor has it that Boss Endo sent some men up there for a job, and they didn't come back. The locals are saying it's a *yokai*."

"Do you believe in them? *Yokai*?" Ikko asked

"It's not that I don't believe *in* them—it's that I don't believe most of the people who say they've seen them. Anyways, we could really make some money with this, you know. Even more than we made in the last town."

"Well, you can count me out," Ikko said. "I'm hungry, but I'd rather be hungry than dead."

A young boy of about seven ran directly out in front of Ikko, and Ikko took him by the shoulders and moved him to the side, out of the way.

"But they're after me," the boy said. He nervously looked back and pointed frantically. Ikko turned and was almost knocked over by two slightly older boys running after the first. They both wore demon masks made of bright red paper. Ikko let out a small scream and jumped back, and all three boys began laughing hysterically, pointing at him.

"Huh. Maybe you aren't the man for the job after all," Hiroji said, without a hint of a smile. He kept walking. Ikko shooed off the boys and jogged a couple steps to catch up with Hiroji.

"Oh, you know I'm just jumpy. Where are the parents, I'd like to know. Kids are running wild these days." He composed himself a bit. "Now what's your stupid plan?"

***

"My name is Hirate Hiroji, and I'd like to speak to Boss Endo," Hiroji said. There were three men in front of Boss Endo's large townhouse. Hiroji sized them up . *Young toughs. Good-for-nothings.* One was standing in the open doorway of the building, chewing a toothpick. He had a long scar on his forehead. He glanced at Hiroji for a moment, and looked away. The other man, short and squat, was pacing back and forth in front of the building. He was talking to himself, and he didn't look up. The third man was smoking a pipe. He walked up to Hiroji, pulled the pipe from his mouth, and blew smoke in Hiroji's face.

"What do you want to see him about?" the man said.

"A job. I think he could use our help," Hiroji said. Ikko stood a few paces behind, and tried to look as confident as Hiroji.

"It's no picnic here," the man said. "Four men got killed just in the last week." He took another draw on his pipe.

"So you've got some openings, then?" Hiroji said.

The man flashed a quick grin. He looked back at Ikko and gave a little snort. He looked down at Hiroji's *katana*, and back up at his expressionless eyes. "Maybe you know what you're doing, maybe not. Not my decision. Wait here."

The man went into the townhouse. Hiroji looked sternly at the other two men, but they didn't make eye contact with him. A few moments later, the man with the pipe came back out.

"Boss Endo will see you now," he said. "I'm Kunio." Hiroji nodded, and Ikko followed suit. They walked up to the doorway and Kunio put his palm out.

"Your sword stays with me while you're in there. You can keep…whatever else you have," Kunio said. Hiroji paused for a second, and then unstrapped his *katana* and scabbard and handed it to Kunio before going in.

***

"So, Hirate Hiroji, you're looking for a job?" Boss Endo said. He was seated on a tatami mat. "Leave us, Kunio." He waved his hand, and Kunio bowed and exited the room.

"Yes, sir. Myself and my partner, Fujima Ikko."

Boss Endo quickly scanned Hiroji from feet to head. "*Ronin*, eh? What happened to your master?"

"Dead," Hiroji said.

Endo nodded. "By your hand?"

"Certainly not," Hiroji said. His back stiffened.

"Good enough, then. What are your skills?"

"Sword, bow, spear, empty hand. The usual."

Endo nodded again. "And your friend?"

Hiroji glanced back at Ikko, who was silent. "He has more...unusual skills. Among other things, he's an exorcist," Hiroji said. Ikko nearly choked, but his expression remained unchanged. Boss Endo looked at Ikko in earnest.

"An *exorcist*? Interesting," Endo said. "Very interesting." He raised his cup of sake and took a sip. "I know the rumors are all around town. What have you heard?

Hiroji paused and rubbed his stubble. "Not much, just that some of your men have been killed, and it may have been a *yokai*."

"You believe in the *yokai*, then?"

Hiroji chuckled and looked over at Ikko. "Do we believe in *yokai*, Ikko?" Ikko stared back blankly. Hiroji laughed with a bit more emphasis and gave Ikko a stern glance. "I should say we do, after what we've been through together, eh?"

Ikko's eyes shifted around the room nervously for a moment, and then he gave out his own hearty laugh. "Oh yes. Yes, the *yokai*! Not a fun bunch to deal with, we can tell you that." Hiroji chuckled again and slapped Ikko on the back. Endo laughed as well, excitedly.

"You've dealt with them, then?" Endo said.

Ikko stepped forward. "Let's just say we've taught a couple of them a few lessons," he said. "Once, I remember we were..." Hiroji slapped his hand down hard on Ikko's shoulder.

"Boss Endo, perhaps you could tell us exactly what happened to your men," Hiroji said.

"Yes, yes. Of course," Endo said. "Would you like some sake? Of course you would. Akiko! Bring some sake. Please you two, sit down."

Akiko was certainly beautiful, and Hiroji wasn't sure if she was Endo's daughter or mistress—he thought it best not to inquire. She brought out sake bowls for Hiroji and Ikko and poured each a drink. Hiroji nodded, and Ikko smiled and bowed his head. Boss Endo waved her away.

"It was just one week ago this evening," Endo said. "I was coming back from dinner—there were many of us out on the streets that night. It was a beautiful early summer evening. I remember the night sky was as clear as could be. Then, without warning, right over our heads shot a meteor, or a comet, I don't know what they call it. It was bright as the sun, and made a loud rushing, whistling noise. The women all screamed. It went straight over the village. *Whoosh*." Endo traced the path in the air with his hand.

"We could see it go right over the trees and into Lake Shinji. We could hear the splash from here in town. There was a hissing, too, like water thrown on a fire," he said.

Ikko listened wide-eyed. Hiroji was nonplussed. He took a sip of his sake. "How did your men die?" Hiroji said.

Boss Endo nodded, continuing his tale. "Well you know, I'm a...businessman, and I have to run my operations. Competition is fierce, let me tell you. You can't let up for a minute."

Hiroji sighed heavily and took another sip.

"I did what any good boss would do," Endo continued. "My rival is Akimoto, as you may know. An awful man. He's been moving in on my territory, and he's got a small little hideout up on the hill by the lake. Some of his men have taken up there, and they've been giving me problems. They've hired a *ronin*, like you. Arima is his name. Good with a *katana*. Too good, for my liking. Not good for my business. Well, I thought I'd take advantage of all the commotion, and send a couple men up to check out the place. I told them not to start any trouble—just scout it out and come back with a report."

"And what did they find?" Ikko asked.

"Well, they never came back," Endo said. "It should have only taken them a few hours. Four at most. After six hours, I sent two more men up, including Chisaka, my best swordsman. I told him to do what he had to do. None of Akimoto's men could have stood up to him—not even Arima."

"And?" Hiroji asked.

Boss Endo shrugged. "He and the other man didn't come back either."

"So Akimoto's men got the better of yours? It happens, you know," Hiroji said.

"No," Endo said. "I have a low-level spy in with Akimoto. He sent word that only one of Akimoto's men from the hideout made it back, and he was barely sane. He said he'd seen everyone killed, including Arima and Chisaka, and that he had only just made it out alive. He kept going on about *yokai*. He ran out on Akimoto the next day, and never returned."

"So how do we fit into this?" Hiroji asked. "What would you want us to do?"

"Don't you see?" Endo said. "They didn't kill each other—something killed all of them. Something, I'm thinking, that maybe you're familiar with." He looked Ikko in the eye.

"So you want us to go up there and...dispatch whatever it was?

Boss Endo leaned in, and Ikko did as well. "Look, I need to know what really happened up there. If Akimoto's man Arima is still alive, and I've lost Chisaka—I'm in trouble. But even if Chisaka is lost, as long as Arima is dead my forces are stronger than Akimoto's. Don't you see? I can take advantage of that, and get Akimoto out of the picture for good." Boss Endo's smile was devious, and it gave Ikko a slight shiver up his spine.

Hiroji sat back, and took another sip of sake. Ikko looked nervously at Hiroji, and then took a sip from his own cup.

"Why don't you just send your own local men? Why hire outsiders?" Hiroji asked.

Boss Endo sighed and shook his head. "My men are mostly simple types—superstitious, country folk. They're spooked, to be honest with you. They're not cowards, mind you—they're good in a fight, but they say they'll only fight men."

"What are you offering us?" Hiroji said. He knew now that the deal would be made.

"Ten *ryō* now, ten when you return," Endo said.

"Each," Hiroji said. Endo started to protest, then grimaced, and nodded.

"What kind of proof do you want? I'm sure you're not going to pay us to pretend to go up there and come back the next day with a false story."

Boss Endo smiled. "Akimoto's man Arima has a possession he's well-known for: a foreign pocket watch. They say it's very old, but was well-crafted and still works. Bring that back to me, and you'll get the rest of your money. *If* you come back." He smiled that same unpleasant smile again.

Hiroji bowed, and Ikko and Endo followed suit. The three of them stood up.

Boss Endo nudged Ikko. "Hey, what do you think it is?"

"Huh?" Ikko said.

Boss Endo was impatient. "What kind of *yokai*? Goblin, demon, ogre?"

"Oh," Ikko said. He frantically tried to think of something to say. "Well…it really could be…any number of *yokai*. This time of year, this region…won't really know until we get up there. But don't worry, whatever it is, it's his unlucky day!" Ikko flashed a big grin, and Boss Endo laughed heartily and slapped him on the back.

"Anything you need from me?" Boss Endo asked.

Hiroji nodded. "I saw a bow and some arrows on the way in," he said. Endo nodded.

"And you, Ikko?"

"Oh, uh…yes…a spear would be nice."

Boss Endo smiled and nodded enthusiastically. "You'll have it." He called to his top man. "Kunio, lead these men out, if you would. Give them what they ask for. And give them each ten *ryō*." Hiroji and Ikko picked up the bow and spear, and Kunio returned Hiroji's *katana.*

***

"Ten *ryō*!" Ikko said. He could barely contain his excitement as he half-skipped down the main street. They passed by an old woman playing the shamisen, and Ikko dropped a coin in her bowl. He couldn't stop grinning. "What are we going to do? How about a big dinner? All the works, sake and women all night. Some grilled fish, Shijimi clams, big bowls of noodles?"

"You want to enjoy your last meal, is that it?" Hiroji said, his pace firm and steady as usual.

"Huh? Last meal? What are you talking about? We're not

really going up there, are we?"

"What are you scared of? You're the exorcist. You've dispatched lots of *yokai*," Hiroji said.

Ikko shook his head in a mixture of frustration and disbelief, struggling to get his words out. "Look, we've got ten *ryō*—we can live for a long time on that. Why don't we just take off? Screw Endo and his stupid gangster war."

"We can get a lot more than ten *ryō* out of this," Hiroji said. He stopped walking and Ikko bumped into him. Hiroji turned and gave Ikko a stern glance. They were standing in front of the cart of the woman selling rice balls. Hiroji gestured towards the woman with his upturned palm.

"What?" Ikko said.

"This is your fancy dinner," Hiroji said.

"Oh, no. Not rice balls for dinner," Ikko said, scrunching up his face.

"You were just saying how much you wanted one, not more than an hour ago," Hiroji said.

"Yeah, but that was when we didn't have any money," Ikko said.

"Get enough for me too, and pack them up. We'll eat on the way," Hiroji said, and started walking towards the hills. Hiroji moved quickly, but for a good two minutes he could still hear Ikko complaining and arguing with the woman over the price of the rice balls.

***

It was still early afternoon as they made their way out of town. It had been a rainy spring, but it had been fairly dry over the last week. The well-traveled dirt road was dusty, but the grass and leaves on the trees were the bright green of early summer. They passed the occasional traveler, one samurai on horseback, and one elderly woman with a basket of kindling wood on her back. Then they came upon a traveling troupe of acrobats, actors and musicians on their way into town. Their brightly painted wooden cart advertised their traveling show. Hiroji and Ikko stepped off to the side of the road to let the troupe pass.

"Thank you, sirs," yelled an elderly man riding in the cart, waving. Ikko waved back.

"That's what I should have been. Traveling musician. I can sing, play the drum. It'd be a lot safer than taking crazy jobs like this, that's for sure," Ikko said.

"Nobody's forcing you to stay," Hiroji said.

"Oh, I feel *sorry* for you, that's why I stay," Ikko said. "What kind of a life would you have without me?"

Hiroji raised his eyebrows and shook his head.

The road continued at a gentle but steady incline. Ikko looked back from the height they had reached and saw that they had a nice view of the town. The sun was shining and the sky was a bright blue, almost cloud-free.

"Ah, it is a nice day, isn't it? Great to feel the sun on your face. Birds are singing." He skipped a couple steps as he looked over at Hiroji. "You know how to use that thing?" he said, pointing at the bow. Hiroji had it unstrung, in a wrapping strapped over his back.

"I do," Hiroji said. He looked over at Ikko, carrying his long spear. "How about you with that spear? I can't imagine you've ever held anything other than a fishing pole."

"Are you kidding?" Ikko said. "My cousin was a master with a spear. We played all the time as kids, and he taught me everything." Hiroji shook his head and let out a small sigh.

***

They walked on for almost two hours, until Hiroji stopped. He took his knapsack off, and pulled out a map.

Ikko got out his water skin and took a drink. He poured some over his face, and wiped off the sweat. It wasn't that hot out, but it was humid and he had been walking mostly uphill.

"This a good place for lunch?" Ikko asked.

"Sure," Hiroji said. He looked at the map, and then turned his body to orient himself in the right direction. "We've been traveling west. And this road turns north, towards Mt. Asahi. We're going to break off here, and head south, to Lake Shinji. We're not that far from where Endo said the Akimoto hideout was." Hiroji sat down, and Ikko tossed him the water skin. Hiroji caught it and took a long drink, and then took one of the rice balls that Ikko handed him.

"So, we should be able to get there in a half hour or so, huh?" Ikko said. He looked up into the bright sunny sky. "We've got lots of time, then. No hurry."

"Of course, the longer we stop, the fewer hours of daylight we're going to have. I have to say, I'm not as good a shot with this bow at night," Hiroji said. He took another long, slow drink from the water skin.

Ikko shoved the rest of his rice ball in his mouth, stood up with his pack and picked up his spear. "Let's go then, no need to lollygag here," Ikko said.

Hiroji shrugged as he slowly finished his rice ball.

***

The late afternoon sun was still fairly high as they found the path to the Akimoto hideout. It wasn't well-worn, but it had been traveled recently. They came through a clearing of trees when Hiroji grabbed Ikko's shoulder and pulled him back behind a large pine. Hiroji put his finger to his lips, and pointed ahead. Ikko peeked out cautiously from behind the tree, and saw what Hiroji had noticed. It was the hideout. Ikko quickly pulled his head back behind the tree, and looked at Hiroji. Hiroji motioned for Ikko to lean in so he could whisper to him.

"I'm going to circle around, and if it looks clear, I'm going in. You just wait here, and don't move. You come when I tell you," Hiroji said. Ikko nodded quickly. It sounded like a good plan, he thought. A safe plan, which didn't involve him doing much of anything. Exactly the kind of plan he liked.

Staying behind the trees, Hiroji crouched as he made his way to the front of the hideout, which was really nothing more than a good-sized cabin built on the hill, with a large storage shed next to it. The cabin was only a few meters from the lake shore, and it was well-situated, Hiroji thought. It was easy to see anyone coming across the lake by boat, and with a lookout or two, it would also be fairly easy to spot anyone approaching by land. Apparently, there were no lookouts today. The cabin door was slightly ajar. He observed the whole scene for several minutes. There was no sign of any activity, or people. Hiroji slowly drew his *katana.* Ikko watched from behind his tree as Hiroji came out of the woods and strode quickly and silently to the front door of the cabin. With one motion he kicked in the door and disappeared inside. Ikko's heart was pounding, and he noticed that his hands were sweating as he tightly held his spear. He listened for commotion or yells. He looked for Hiroji or someone else to come rushing out of the door. Nothing.

After a minute, Hiroji slowly came back out the door, scratching the back of his head. He looked over at Ikko, and shrugged his shoulders. Ikko came out from behind the trees, alert, tense and brandishing his spear. He walked, rotating, looking in every direction as he made his way over to Hiroji.

"What's in there?" Ikko asked.

"Go look for yourself," Hiroji said.

Ikko thought for a second, looked around, and then went into the cabin, spear in hand. A good deal of light was coming in from the back window, and Ikko surveyed the big room. It was empty. On the main table were a few plates and bowls, and a half-full pot of rice porridge. It looked to be no more than a day old.

"Nobody here," Hiroji said, as he came back in.

"Looks like they left in a hurry," Ikko said. He picked up a bowl, sniffed it, and took a drink. "Didn't even finish their sake," he said.

"Hope they didn't all die from poisoning," Hiroji said. Ikko ignored him, and took another long sip from the bowl.

"Eh, there are worse ways to go," Ikko said, and he downed the last of the sake. "So, we checked the place out. We didn't find anything, can't get what's-his-name's pocket watch to take back. We've got our ten *ryō*, let's move on."

"Let's look around a bit more. Aren't you even curious as to what happened?" Hiroji asked.

"No, I'm not," Ikko said.

They walked back outside, and Hiroji went over to the door of the storage shed and opened it.

"Hey, Ikko. Look at this," Hiroji said. Ikko walked over and looked in.

"What? I don't see anything," Ikko said.

"Look up," Hiroji said, pointing towards the ceiling with his *katana*. Hanging from the ceiling, by their feet, were men—bodies—partially wrapped in some type of...cocoon, it almost seemed to Hiroji. There were eight or nine of them.

"What...what the hell is that?" Ikko said. Hiroji walked over to the closest body, and felt the cocoon. It was greenish, and more wet and sticky than a regular spider's web. Still, it pulled away fairly easily from the body, and it came off in big clumps. The man was dead, no doubt about that. His face was shriveled and dried like leather—even though Hiroji knew he probably hadn't been dead more than a couple days.

"I'm guessing this is Chisaka," Hiroji said, as he pulled the upside-down man's knife out of its scabbard and examined it. "An ordinary gangster doesn't have a *tanto* of this quality. And he's got

Endo's patch on his sleeve."

"Yeah, that's great. Let's get out of here," Ikko said. "Wait...What's that?" He saw a glint of glass and metal on the floor. He walked over and bent down to look. It was a fine western pocket watch. "Hey hey!" Ikko said as he looked it over, and put it to his ear. "Still ticking. All right, we've got everything, and can get our ten more *ryō*!"

They walked out of the storage shed when the sound of splashing water came from the lake.

"What was that?" Ikko said.

Hiroji shook his head angrily for Ikko to be quiet, and strained to listen. He slowly brought his *katana* up and to the ready. Hiroji got the sense of some large thing rushing towards him, but all he saw was a flash of a dark gray body with a white underbelly. It had many legs, or tentacles—Hiroji wasn't sure which. It moved silently through the trees and with a speed Hiroji would not have thought possible for such a large creature. It had to be the size of a cow, a bull even. Hiroji raised his sword, but before he could slash down the thing was on them. It slammed into both of them, knocking them to the ground.

Hiroji was able to hold onto his sword, and he got to his feet just in time to face a flurry of tentacles reaching and grabbing for him. The thing had two eyes—black, big eyes—and they looked as lifeless as glass. It had a sort of beak, almost like a squid, but it didn't exactly seem like a sea creature; it moved too easily on land. Hiroji staggered back, and made two powerful slashes with his *katana*. The thing's tentacles were like some sort of tough rubber; they seemed to absorb Hiroji's cuts and bounce them away. He tried a thrust at the thing's head, but the tentacles kept him out of range. Through the whole attack, the *yokai* was perfectly silent.

Hiroji made several more powerful slashes that would have cut a man in two, but with no better results. One tentacle wrapped around his waist, and pulled him in closer. Another wrapped up his sword arm, and constricted enough that the pain caused him to drop his *katana*. The thing threw Hiroji on his back, and then hovered over him. As the beak opened, he could see a snake-like proboscis emerging. Hiroji wasn't sure exactly what the creature was doing, but he was fairly certain he was going to end up like the men hanging in the storage shed. The thing was so powerful; Hiroji could feel his own strength beginning to fade.

"Hey, you! Get off of my friend!" Ikko yelled. Just as his cousin had taught him to do, Ikko drove off of his rooted back foot, and twisted his waist and hips into the thrust. Ikko's spear head went about two feet into the rubbery body of the creature, and it let out a gurgling, high-pitched croak. It lifted itself off of Hiroji and turned around sharply, wrenching the spear from Ikko's hands. Two of the thing's tentacles frantically grasped for the spear, still stuck in its body. Both appendages grasped it and pulled, but they seemed to be working against each other; they simply snapped the shaft of the spear off, leaving the head still embedded. The thing scurried off back into the woods, towards the water.

Then, nothing. The only sounds were the birds chirping in the trees, and Ikko's heavy breathing. Ikko snapped out of his momentary shock and looked to his partner.

"Hiroji!" Ikko yelled, and ran over to his friend. Hiroji got to his knees, and then reached over to pick up his *katana*.

"I'm all right," Hiroji said, rubbing the back of his neck. "Say, I guess your cousin really did teach you the spear."

"What did I tell you? Did you think I'm the kind of person to make that up?" Ikko said. "But shit, let's get out of here. That really *was* a *yokai*! I don't know what the hell kind—spider, octopus—something. Mark my word, this is the last time I ever go looking for them!"

Hiroji got to his feet. "We're not leaving until that thing is dead. I used to be a samurai. I'm not going to run away because I'm scared."

"Well, good luck then, because I am," Ikko said. "And how do you know you can kill it? These things are demons."

"Can't you be a man, for once?" Hiroji said.

"I *am* a man, a *live* man—and I want to keep it that way."

"Look," Hiroji said. "It's probably not going to let us escape, anyways." He unstrapped the bow from his back. "I'm sure those low-life gangsters tried to run away, too. Look where they ended up." He strung the bow and opened up the quiver. He pulled out an arrow, looked down the shaft to check its straightness, and put his finger to the razor sharp point.

"I still think we should just leave," Ikko said.

"You saw it move. If it's not dead, you know we can't outrun it. Better to stay and fight," Hiroji said. Ikko wasn't so sure.

"You go down there, in the direction it went," Hiroji said.

"I'm not going down there," Ikko said. "I don't even have my spear anymore."

"You're not going to need it. When it chases you, just run back here so I can get a clear shot at its head," Hiroji said.

"*When it chases me?* So I'm just bait, now? Why don't you just put me on a hook and cast me over there?" Ikko said.

"The sooner you get started, the sooner we can get out of here. Look, the sun's starting to go down," Hiroji said.

Against his better judgment, Ikko walked away from the cabin and towards the lake, where they saw the thing go. The closer he got to the lake, the slower he stepped. He just got to the point where he could see the lake, and he stopped. He looked, but he didn't see anything. He listened, but there was only silence. He was just about to turn back when something caught his eye. He looked down, and it was the head of his spear. *The thing had managed to pull it out.* Ikko didn't think any more about it: he turned and ran full speed back towards Hiroji. He heard the crash of brush and knew it was on his heels. He jumped over a large rock, and ran as fast as he could—as fast as he ever had, he thought afterward. As he passed in front of the cabin, he could feel the *yokai* right behind him.

Hiroji notched his arrow and drew the bow back quickly. He tracked the thing that was after his friend, gauged its speed and let loose his first arrow. It was a direct hit to the thing's head, right behind the flailing tentacles. Ikko kept running, but the *yokai* was stopped in its tracks. Hiroji quickly notched a second arrow, and let that fly as well. It was as accurate as the first one. As he calmly walked towards the creature, he continued drawing and shooting his long bow. He put another, then another arrow into it. By the time he reached it, six arrows had found their mark in the *yokai*'s head. It seemed to be dead, but Hiroji didn't take any chances. Without the protection of the tentacles, its bulbous head with the terrible beak was exposed. Hiroji drew his *katana*, and with one powerful stroke he cut the thing's head off. He flicked the blood off his blade, and in one deft motion put his *katana* back in its scabbard.

Ikko came running back. “That was fantastic!” He looked down at the body of the thing, and kicked it. “Chase me, will you? What did you get for that? Huh? How did that work out?” He kicked it again, and then turned back to his partner.

“Hiroji, my friend, that was the most incredible thing I’ve ever seen. You’re quite a man. You killed a *yokai*.”

“I had some help,” Hiroji said.

Ikko shrugged and grinned. He pulled out the pocket watch and looked at it. “And this is going to be worth another ten *ryō*,” he said.

“We’re not taking that back,” Hiroji said.

“What do you mean we’re not taking it back?” Ikko asked. “Boss Endo said he’d give us the rest of the money.”

“The only thing Boss Endo would give us is a knife in the back. He can’t have it get around that his men were too scared to come up here, and he had to hire outsiders to do it. Nobody knows us here; nobody would be looking for us. He’d kill us, get his 20 *ryō* back, and then he’d finish off Akimoto, knowing that his rival’s best swordsman was dead. We were expendable from the beginning, Ikko,” Hiroji said.

Ikko slowly frowned. “That son of a bitch. So we’re out our money? Why did we even come up here if you never planned on going back?”

“What is this place, Ikko?” Hiroji said.

“It’s…Akimoto’s hideout?” Ikko said, puzzled.

"If everyone is dead at a gangsters' hideout, don't you think there's probably a pretty good stash of money somewhere in that cabin?" Hiroji said. Ikko's eyes lit up, and a slow smile spread across his face.

***

The next day was sunny with a bright blue sky, and Hiroji and Ikko headed north on the dusty road towards Mt. Asahi and the town on the other side. Ikko's pack was quite a bit heavier than it had been yesterday, but not so heavy that it kept him from skipping every now and then as he walked along on the dusty road with his friend Hiroji.

Thoughts of Water

"It doesn't make any sense," Wade Kelleher said. He had been a rancher his whole life, and in his fifty-five years, he didn't recall any situation as strange as what had been going on the last few days. And this was the kicker. The ten-foot wooden water trough for the horses was now just five wooden planks lying flat on the ground, as if somebody had smashed it apart with a sledgehammer while standing in the middle of it. And the funny thing was that the ground around it was dusty and dry as a bone.

"I'm sure that was near full last night," Wade said, scratching his forehead.

"You think it was them McAllister boys, boss?" Jimmy Doane was Wade's foreman. At only twenty-five, he was younger than several of the ranch hands he managed, but he was confident and didn't have any problem with that—and neither did the men under him.

"No footprints, Jimmy," Wade said, pointing to the ground as he made a half circle in the dirt with the toe of his boot. "And we would have heard any horses."

Jimmy looked down to the dirt and slowly rubbed the back of his neck. "...yeah. And really, what's the point of breakin' up this trough? I mean, if they wanted to kill the horses, they could have just poisoned it or somethin'. And it still don't explain why the cattle ain't been drinkin'."

“The other boys didn’t say anything before they left yesterday? Nothing odd?” Wade asked. Danny, Jay and Rodney had left the previous morning to go buy some cattle down south, and they wouldn’t be back until tomorrow.

“They didn’t say nothin’ to me,” Jimmy said. “They left a little after ten, nothin’ unusual. They were laughin’ and lookin’ forward to a night in town.”

“I don’t know,” Wade said. He took his hat off and wiped the sweat from his forehead. The West Texas sun was already hot, and it was still a while before they’d hit the main heat of the day. “Maybe the herd got some disease, makes them not want to drink...but I’ve never heard of it. Well, let’s you and me go down and check out the river, at least. Maybe there’s something keeping them away from the water....I don’t know. I’m plumb out of ideas.”

The river was about a mile ride from the barn, down a grassy slope, and by the time they got there it was a little after noon.

The rain had been heavy that spring, and there had been a couple of odd storms—heavy downpours out of a clear blue sky. At any rate, the water level of the river was a little higher than normal for this time of year. That was generally a good thing in a place where the availability of water could make or break a man’s fortunes.

“Would you look at that,” Wade said, as the two approached the river. The several hundred longhorns were spread out along the side of the river, but none were closer than ten yards from the water. They were milling about nervously. Every now and then one would tentatively take a couple steps towards the river and then step back again, mooing plaintively.

“Maybe somethin’ died upstream,” Jimmy said. “Fouled the

water." He rode up to the river's edge and dismounted. He led his horse by the reins as he walked down the last leg of the dusty cow path to the little inlet where the herd usually drank. His horse snorted and whinnied, not wanting to go where its owner was leading.

"What's got into you, boy?" Jimmy said, stroking the horse's neck and mane. "We're just goin' down to the water. You've been here a million times." He kneeled down at the river's bank and cupped a palm full of water. He brought it to his nose and sniffed, and then he drank it. He shrugged his shoulders and turned to Wade. "I don't know, boss. Seems fine to me."

"All right," Wade said. "I'm still going to ride upstream a bit and see if I can find anything." He turned his horse and set off at an easy trot.

It wasn't exactly a scream that came from Jimmy—it was more of a surprised shout. But Wade heard it and turned just in time to see Jimmy scrambling backwards on his rear end, frantically trying to push himself away from the river on his palms and heels. What he saw next, though, was something that Wade Kelleher had no frame of reference for.

The water reached out for Jimmy.

It wasn't a wave, and it didn't take any particular shape, but a mass of water came up onto the bank, overtook Jimmy and enveloped him, and dragged him back towards the river. Jimmy was struggling and crying for help, but he couldn't free himself. With a loud splash he was abruptly pulled into the river and under the surface. Jimmy's horse whinnied and reared up, and in a panic it turned and made its way back up the trail and past the longhorns.

"Jimmy!" Wade yelled. He turned the reins and in no time he

had galloped the thirty yards over to where Jimmy had been. He swung down quickly off his horse and ran to the water's edge. The river was flowing at its normal, easy pace and there were just a few gentle ripples on the surface where Jimmy had gone in. Wade frantically looked down into the water, his eyes darting back and forth. About five yards out he spotted the figure of Jimmy, still struggling frantically under the clear water. But he was moving away rapidly. *Moving upstream*.

"What the hell?" Wade said, half whispering to himself. "Jimmy!" he yelled. Wade could still see the dark vest of his foreman under the water, and he tried to keep one eye on Jimmy as he ran upstream along the bank, keeping pace. The water wasn't more than eight or ten feet deep, but Wade couldn't believe how fast Jimmy was moving—as if something unseen was dragging him. In a flash, Jimmy was far enough away that the water was refracting the light, and Wade couldn't tell anymore if Jimmy was still fighting or not. It became clear to Wade that he couldn't catch up, and Jimmy was beyond help.

Wade fell to one knee and put his left palm on the ground, gasping for breath. He was more than a few years past his prime, and it had been a while since he had run at full speed like that for any distance. He was still trying to process what was happening when he looked up and saw it. Another shapeless formation of water was emerging from the surface of the river right in front of him. It pushed to the bank and onto land, and it advanced towards him. It was moving fast, but Wade was a quick man in his youth, and the old reflexes kicked in. He leaped back just enough to avoid the writhing bulk of water that reached for his leg. He turned and ran away from the river, and as he looked back he saw the water that had attacked him withdrawing back to the river, as if it had extended itself as far as it could.

Wade rode hard back up towards the ranch, trying to make sense of what had just happened. He'd go into the house and pour himself a whiskey, for starters. Maybe a double. Then he'd think things through. There had to be some reasonable explanation, and he'd figure it out when he calmed down.

He was within fifty yards of the ranch house when he first felt it. Something was hitting his side, right under his ribs. At first it was just few taps, but then it started to hit harder. Again and again, on his right side, until he felt like an overmatched boxer on the receiving end of a series of body shots. Wade was already shaken up, but when he turned and looked down he couldn't see anything. He kept riding, but then the next hit felt like a hammer, and it knocked him off the horse. His hat flew off and he hit the ground hard, and his face went into a patch of grass and warm dust that had been baking under the noontime sun. He felt another punch on his side, and another. He winced in pain, and then he looked down and saw what it was. *His canteen.* His whole body jerked in surprise. He sat up and frantically pulled the canteen's leather strap over his head and off his shoulder, and with fear and rage he swung it like David's sling against Goliath. He threw the almost full canteen a good forty-five feet. The canteen continued to flop and jump wildly on the ground, haphazardly trying to make its way back towards Wade.

His horse Tagger had stayed close—he was always a good horse—and Wade got up and grabbed the pommel, put a foot up into the stirrup and swung back into the saddle. He rode hard, and when he came up to the porch of his ranch house, he paused and looked back towards the river. Then he thought of the big cistern out just behind the back door, which was still about two-thirds full.

Tagger whinnied and paced nervously. Wade Kelleher decided that he might better get that whiskey in town, and he turned his horse and kept riding.

A Better Fence

Captain Harrier took off his cap and wiped the sweat from his brow, and he peered across the canyons and the dull blue sand of the desert that stretched out to the horizon. Huge, strangely shaped rock monoliths of red and faded gold dotted the landscape, haphazardly placed like some ancient race of giants frozen in mid-stride. Yu-tab was really a beautiful planet, Harrier thought. Its pale green sky and single sun and moon made it enough like Earth to be comfortable, but just different enough to be exotic and alluring, if one had a romantic outlook about such things. Harrier seemed to remember that he used to be the romantic type, years ago. Or maybe a lifetime ago. At any rate it was before this war with the Jurona, and before he had seen men under his command die, like the two who were killed last night.

Harrier was a young forty. He had the weathered face of a man who had lived comfortably out-of-doors for many of those years, but with his share of the aches and pains that such a life inevitably brings. He took a drink from his canteen, and looked again out into the desert. Still nothing. He didn't bother looking through his electroview, because he knew it would show the same thing, just the basic fauna of a few sand lizards, scavenger bats, blue rock snakes, and other more or less harmless animals. There would be no sign of what attacked his men last night.

"Captain," Private Hajima called to him. "Friendly approaching." Hajima pointed back out behind their small compound with the barrel of his flash rifle.

Captain Harrier looked towards the Yu-tabi village of Jn'rez, almost a kilometer from their small base. A single Yu-tabi male approached across the blue sands, and Harrier recognized the distinctive, calm stride of Balon. Harrier liked Balon as well as he liked any of the Yu-tabi, and that was saying something, because he really did like the Yu-tabi They took some getting used to, no doubt about that. They were humanoid, and could have almost passed for men except for a few things. First and most obviously, they were tall, almost nine feet, and quite thin. Their skin was a deep red. And their voices—it was really difficult to describe their voices if you hadn't heard one speak. They were quite adept at languages, and could learn English without much difficulty when they wanted to. But when they spoke it was almost like a voice coming through a musical instrument, like a cello or an oboe. It was unnerving the first time you heard it, but Harrier got used to it pretty quickly.

The smell was something else, though. It wasn't pleasant, and it wasn't unpleasant—nobody had come up with an English word to describe it, and most who spent time with the Yu-tabi didn't even try. But it was there, all the time. Still, Harrier liked them.

In centuries past, the Yu-tabi had fought amongst themselves; clan against clan, and city-state against city-state, but none living today could recall the last time Yu-tabi had fought each other—and their lifespan was more than 250 Earth years. Now, they were mostly craftsman and farmers in small settlements, and they seemed to be quite a religious people; they made Harrier's job easy.

After the Jurona had begun using Yu-tab as a minor staging and supply base, the Union of Greater Earth had launched phase artillery strikes from space. They got the Juronan base all right, but they also caused a number of civilian casualties in a nearby Yu-tabi village. That was bad publicity for the UGE, and with public support for the war with the Jurona already tepid, the politicians were big on humanitarian relief efforts. That suited Harrier just fine—always better to help people than kill them, he thought. And even better when they're not trying to kill *you*. Harrier also thought that it was a hell of a lot easier to deal with the natives one-on-one on a remote planet like this, without a lot of government and military bureaucracy and red tape getting in the way.

"Orders, Captain?" Hajima asked, his flash rifle at the ready as Balon came closer. They all knew Balon was no threat, but Hajima followed protocol.

"Let him pass," Harrier said. Hajima waved at Balon, and motioned the tall Yu-tabi into the compound. Harrier walked over and extended his hand to Balon, who took it.

"My friend Harr-ierrrr," Balon said, putting his hand on Harrier's shoulder. "I am sorry to heeeear of your men's death last niiiiight. We will pray to N'wei for their spirits to beeee saved. Were theyyyy men of faith?"

Harrier shook his head, and looked up at the russet-red face of Balon. "I'm afraid not," he said.

Balon nodded, and looked out to the desert. "But whoooo knows what faith....one has in seeecret? Only N'wei can judge."

"Balon," Harrier said, "I need your help."

"I knowwwww you do, and that is why I come."

"You called them, what? Molch...?" Harrier said, trying to remember the name.

"Molche'ne. They are demons. Theyyyyy come in the night, as I told you," Balon said. He adjusted the oddly shaped cloth cap on his head, and shielded his eyes with his hand to block the sun as he looked out over the desert. "As I have tollld you, you willlll not see them out therrrre...in daylight."

"But they're physical creatures, though, right? I can't figure out why they didn't register on our sensor perimeter," Harrier said. "Don't they attack your villages? How do the Yu-tabi stop them?"

Balon smiled that detached smile that Harrier still found hard to read and slightly unnerving. "They can be physical. Your men were...torn apart, no? Yu-tabi don't always stop themmmm. Weeee don't always know why they come. But we don't stop fighting them."

"That's what I'm asking—how do you fight them?" Harrier was getting impatient. The Yu-tabi were intelligent, but they didn't seem to be able to answer any straight question with a straight answer.

"We pray to N'wei. We read N'wei's words. We live the way N'wei has decreeeeed. We....your language is small...*honor* our brothers. Even strange brothers, like youuuuu," Balon said.

"I don't understand," Harrier said.

Balon smiled again. "It is sometimes said that the molche'ne must beeee...summoned...*desired*, before they willlll come to a man. Many ages ago, sommmmme Yu-tabi worshiped and followed the molche'ne."

"And what happened to them?" Harrier asked. He had to play along now, out of politeness if nothing else. The Yu-tabi valued manners above almost everything.

"They became a very rich, powerful tribe. Until theyyyy were devoured, by the molche'ne they worshipped," Balon said.

Harrier took another drink of water from his canteen. He offered the canteen to Balon, who ignored him. The Yu-tabi could drink plain water, but they didn't like the taste. Harrier knew this, but he didn't want to be discourteous.

"Look, Balon," Harrier said. "I appreciate your advice, and I mean no disrespect to your faith. But I'm interested in their physical characteristics. I have my perimeter fence sensors set to pick up the Jurona, your people, mine, and anything else that might be on this planet. If I know more about these creatures, I'm sure my equipment can detect them. Look, your people have benefited from some of our scanners and electroviews. You use technology, you know what I'm talking about."

"Harrierrrr, when you first came I told you about the molche'ne, and your...technology...said they were not reeeeal. That Yu-tabi dream themmm, you told us," Balon said. His tone was factual, not accusatory.

"I know, I was wrong," Harrier said. "But now that I know they're real, we have the equipment to defend ourselves—and to defend your people as well, Balon."

Balon shook his head. "Your people know N'wei, even if you call himmmmm by another name. I can offer you no other help."

***

It was almost sundown, and Harrier gave one final briefing to Privates Hajima and Soren. They had spent most of the day examining the evidence of the previous attack, and Harrier felt he had a better idea of what they were dealing with.

"Listen, men, just be calm and have faith in our planning. We've gone through the tapes from last night, and I *know* we've got the density signature on those things now. I can see why they didn't register. The fence sensors have all been re-calibrated—there's no way anything is getting in here tonight. And even if they do, there's nothing on this planet that can stand up to our flash rifles. Jacobs and Savard weren't expecting anything last night—we *are*, and forewarned is forearmed. Now get to your posts, and stay in contact," Harrier said. Hajima and Soren nodded and hurried to their respective positions.

It was a few hours after sundown that Hajima's voice came over the comlink. The words were jumbled, panicked.

"Captain, I've got something here. It's (unintelligible)—I think...! IT'S THROUGH THE PERIMITER!" The high pitched whine of a flash rifle sounded, and then the comlink went dead.

"Hold your position, Hajima! Lay down fire!" Harrier shouted, as he frantically checked the remote stats on the fence monitor.

Balon stood watch on the edge of his village, with his young son by his side. They both looked out through the dark night to the Earthmen's outpost in the distance. They could hear shouts and screams, and see the blue-white streaks of the pulses from the flash rifles. Then there was silence, and darkness. Nothing.

Balon mourned his friend, Captain Harrier, and he said a silent prayer to N'wei.

Made in the USA
Middletown, DE
23 August 2016